EBURY PRESS
TAKE NO. 2020

Puneet Sikka is a media professional who has previously worked as a writer in the news and advertising industry. She is also an aspiring actress with performances in theatre, TV and digital commercials, short films as well as a feature film to her name. Puneet studied at the Lady Shri Ram College, Delhi and Symbiosis Institute of Media and Communication, Pune. Her debut novel, *Take No. 2020*, is a hybrid of pop culture and realism that combines her lived experience within the entertainment industry and her passion for writing.

TAKE NO. 2020

2020

~ The Mother of All Retakes ~

~ A NOVEL BY ~

PUNEET SIKKA

EBURY PRESS

An imprint of Penguin Random House

EBURY PRESS

Ebury Press is an imprint of the Penguin Random House group of companies
whose addresses can be found at global.penguinrandomhouse.com

Published by Penguin Random House India Pvt. Ltd
4th Floor, Capital Tower 1, MG Road,
Gurugram 122 002, Haryana, India

First published in Ebury Press by Penguin Random House India 2024

ISBN 9780143466741

Typeset in Sabon by MAP Systems, Bengaluru, India

www.penguin.co.in

Contents

III. Cut!

I

Lights, Camera!

Prologue

(Scene #1, Shot #1) Take #4

Sometime in 2018 B.C. (Before Covid-19)

The cab has left the busy highway behind. After a few zigzags, it turns into a secluded lane that narrows to a bumpy and dusty road. There is ample daylight at 5.30 p.m., yet Meera feels ill at ease. She reaches for her phone to confirm the address.

'Yes, ma'am. It is an automobile company's warehouse. We are using it as a makeshift audition space. If you are on the dirt track, you're on the right track. Keep following the road till you reach a black gate. Let security know the purpose of your visit. Drive straight in. I'll meet you at the reception,' the casting assistant says.

When Meera walks into the lobby, the clickety-clack of her heels bounces off the walls. There isn't a soul in sight except for a wiry, acne-faced young man. He introduces himself as Arun and greets her so chivalrously that it makes her wonder if he is hiding a sinister motive. He leads the way to an enclosed area the size of a football field. She asks about the unusual location.

'This short film is part of a digital series being sponsored by an automobile company. The brand decided to host auditions in their own warehouse. Since they use this space to record car stunt videos for YouTube, it made sense to test actors driving actual cars instead of simulating the action. The company is a stickler for performance, you see,' Arun smiles innocently at her. He has, perhaps, already repeated this story a few times. She notices that though he's chatty, he is keenly watching her every gesture. A slight shiver runs down her spine. This was a mistake. She shouldn't have come here all by herself. But this is Keval Jha's casting. He wouldn't be so openly nefarious unless these guys were masquerading as The Keval Jha. People did that so often. Oh gosh, how had she fallen for this?

'How many actors have you auditioned for the role so far?'

'You are the third actor we are auditioning today. It is a very limited audition,' Arun says.

'Limited audition' would have made her chuckle had she not been getting the creeps. She continues to keep a composed expression as she weighs her alternatives. Her phone isn't detecting any cabs nearby. She regrets letting go of her taxi. Beads of sweat begin to form near her temples. She dabs at her forehead with the back of her palm. Patchy make-up is the least of her concerns right now.

Arun walks back to her with the audition script. She hadn't registered his absence even though she'd seen him walk ahead of her.

'Most of it is action, barely any dialogue,' he says. 'In the scene, the girl is being chased by a black car. She reaches a safe space and crouches to hide. Tired from the chase, her eyes begin to droop. As a shadow falls on her from the back, her eyes snap open.'

Meera turns so pale that if a camera had been recording her right now, she would've bagged the role.

'May . . . may I get a glass of water please?' Her mind is racing and her pulse is racing faster as Arun nods and leaves the room. Something is terribly wrong. She remembers reading about a similar incident a year ago when an aspiring actor was called to a warehouse for an audition and brutally murdered. The killers were never caught. *What if it's the same gang?*

At the first opportunity, she bolts towards the exit door numbered one. It's latched from the outside. Colour drains from her face. She races towards the exit door numbered two which is a few feet away. Locked. There is a third, smaller door but without an exit sign. Praying for it to open and lead her to the main gate, she pulls at it with such force that she almost falls backwards when it opens. It's the maintenance room— dark and musty, its walls are lined with shelves holding dusty tools and supplies. Partially hidden behind the mess, she sees a square wooden board nailed to the wall. Sweeping the tools aside, she hits the thin makeshift board with all her might, which gives way instantly. She pulls out the jagged parts and crawls out into an empty corridor—a fire escape route, perhaps. Her footsteps echo as she runs towards the door at the end of the aisle that says 'main exit'. She turns the handle. It's open!

Out of the door and down the steps on to an uneven, grassy patch, she looks like a fleeting ghost. The sky is unusually dark. How long was she inside the warehouse?

The faceless predator of her childhood nightmares, whom she thought she had long outgrown, comes charging at her, more ferocious than ever. The impending danger quickens her breath as she turns around.

There's no one in sight.

Could the predator be hiding behind that tree with a dried garland around its trunk, or in the dusty van with a flat tyre? She notices a CCTV camera panning the parking lot. The device turns towards her eerily, almost as if it were a pair of eyes tracking her movements.

Meera darts towards the black gate, relieved to find it ajar. She runs out on to the dirt road, hoping to hitch a ride from a passing vehicle. As if on cue, a black SUV is headed in her direction, blinding her with its headlights. She waves frantically, making the car stop a few feet from her. The tightness in her chest loosens a little and a tentative smile appears on her lips. She races towards the vehicle, opens the door and jumps into the passenger seat.

Her body is tingling. She has barely caught her breath when she hears the click of the car's central lock. Her gaze flies to the driver. It is *The Zombie*. Her blood turns to ice.

'Cut! Bravo! Brilliant take!' the director shouts.

Meera is thrilled. She can still feel the goosebumps on her arms as she hugs herself, accepting the director's and crew's congratulations. She had spent the previous night preparing for the shoot: studying the script, pruning her body language, movement and state of mind. Of course, she'd imagined demons of all kinds. It had been the least difficult part, frankly. She has a few of her own pet demons who languish in the shadows.

As she changes out of her costume, she realizes how exhausted she is. It has been a long, hot day. All she wants now is to slip into her pyjamas and get a good night's sleep.

Fortunately, the summer night brings a breeze. Its swooshing muffles the sound of the local train running half a kilometre away. She is staying at one of the old Parsi houses in the Dadar–Matunga area in Mumbai, which the owner has leased to eight other female paying guests apart from her. This building has three more floors above it, and like so many others in this colony, holds an old-world charm with a long corridor-like verandah on the ground floor and wide streets outside with a canopy of trees shading them. These structures are in stark contrast to the usual residential buildings in the suburbs that are just pieces of blocks placed in tall, vertical piles—each a clone of the next, nothing distinctive in their appearance or features. The whirr of the ceiling fan and air conditioner, and a rhythmic, whistling snore from the room next to hers lull Meera to sleep.

The sirens jolt each member of the house awake. The apartment above theirs has caught fire and the building is being evacuated. Somebody screams as a flame bursts through a window, spraying shards of glass on the street below.

The women in the house grab their wallets, phones, laptops, bras—whatever they consider important. Meera picks up a leather-bound diary with tattered edges, and a discoloured black-and-white photo of a smiling young Amma holding her on her first birthday.

Take #1

Once Upon a Take

December 2017 B.C., Chennai

Meera was at her desk when she received the offer to audition in Mumbai for a face wash ad. The brand was launching a national campaign with top Bollywood actress and brand ambassador Sakshi Rai. The prospect of appearing on television commercials, billboards and magazine pages dazzled Meera. It was a dream she was determined not to give up for a dull salaried job.

She was so confident she'd be chosen that she began planning the next five years keeping it in mind. She almost dialled her agency to confirm the audition but decided to think it over again. Would she be able to live away from Patti,[1] who was the very embodiment

---

[1] Paternal grandmother.

of home for her? She was the only family Meera had, the one who had raised her with so much love and care. Meera had struggled with the idea of flying the nest. She had heard stories about young people being gripped by loneliness in big cities like Mumbai, whereas with Patti, there was seldom a dull moment. Sunday evenings were for taking in a play or dance recital, or for an early evening picnic at the beach (the days were unbearably hot), learning how to sew or cook, and, more recently, ambling at Phoenix Marketcity Mall.

Of course, there were times when being with Patti was sheer embarrassment—like when she would break into song as she haggled with the vegetable vendor. Meera would wince and avoid the stares of curious onlookers lest she seem to be with the cuckoo lady. Even so, she couldn't imagine life without Patti.

Then there was Raghu. Her heart ached at the thought of leaving him behind. It had been a glorious seven months of dating him. He seemed like the perfect life partner. Would he consider quitting his corporate job in Chennai and finding one in Mumbai instead so they could move in together? She could pay the bills till he found suitable work. As per her calculations, her fee from this ad would allow her to live in Mumbai for two or three months while visibility from this campaign would open doors for her in the movies. Within no time, she would be inundated with roles, money and more opportunities. Then she, Raghu and Patti could all live together as one happy family.

Had her duties not pulled her away, Meera would have continued building castles in the air. On most days, she punched the keyboard listlessly as she checked routine tasks off her list, till it dawned on her that she had spent her life drifting like a log of wood on a gentle stream. She had switched jobs three times in the last six years; it's as if changing the workplace gave her a sense of movement, and consequently, progress. But she was only going in circles like a hamster on a wheel. The only constant through the years had been her desire to become a full-time actor. Why had she never acted on her acting dream? True, she had signed up with the first agency she'd found, but if acting was where her heart was, she had to make a definitive choice—either maintain the status quo in Chennai with her job and the talent agency or move to Mumbai and start afresh, focusing only on auditions and acting workshops.

Her annual contract with the agency was up for renewal, which was probably what had spurred them into action. They had a lock-in period of six months, after which she could discontinue the relationship if she so wished. And wish it she did. She had come very close to terminating the agreement on two previous occasions. So, when she rapped the agency on its knuckles, they came up with this audition, and pursuing it felt like the obvious choice to make. Besides, she could always figure out her next steps in Mumbai.

Meera phoned the talent agency to confirm the audition. Hope bloomed inside of her but a cloud of scepticism also appeared. Then she thought, it was, after all, only an audition. If it didn't work out, she could always return and pick up from where she had left off. Surely she'd find a company elsewhere looking to fill a vacancy in human resources, if not the same as the one she was currently at. She wanted to avoid dwelling on the downside of a failed attempt in Mumbai lest it make her pessimistic and keep her stuck in the rut.

* * *

2018 B.C., Mumbai

The waiting room is abuzz with gossip about Sakshi Rai and her faux pas at a recent talk show. Riding on the success of her fifth consecutive super-hit film, she had ridiculed a rival's unflattering body shape.

'No wonder this campaign about body positivity was cooked up within a month of the controversy. Why do you think the brand suddenly wants dusky, chubby, curly-haired women flanking Sakshi?' a model says in low tones.

'It's all a whitewash campaign, meant to make Sakshi look more inclusive and to offset the beating her brand image has taken owing to the backlash in the media. Ironically, the duskier you are, the better,' another one adds.

'I even applied extra bronzer to look the part!' confesses a third.

The trio chuckle as they scan the models streaming in through the front door, until one of them says, 'This could take all day. I don't want to miss my audition at

Mickey Taneja's studio later today because I'm waiting for my turn here. It's not every day that one gets a call from his casting office, and that too for a primary character. Another hour, tops, and I'm out of here.'

Someone scurries out of the studio and thunders, 'Silence! There is an audition in progress.'

As the door shuts, the noise level in the studio drops. Meera reminds herself to show her right profile more. She runs a white feather down her cheek, its fronds tickling her. Her au naturel make-up hides the pigmentation on her skin. If only her skin tone were as even as Sakshi Rai's! Though for that, she'll have to know the best dermatologists in town and have a bank account to match.

It is the third take of her audition. The casting supervisor is irritated by the disturbances but speaks calmly. 'Remember to turn your chin sideways as you say your line. We'll do another take.'

He leans in further, holding his knees as she runs the feather down her cheek and mouths the tag line: *Be who you are!* and finishes with an alluring smile. There's something about Meera's vulnerability that evokes his compassion. He cannot point out exactly what it is about her, but she glows with a raw appeal rarely seen in newcomers these days. Off camera, she has the awkwardness of a fawn standing up on its trembling legs for the first time; on camera, the resoluteness of a solitary swan coasting on the water.

If only he could tell her not to get her hopes up and that she wouldn't be the chosen face because the campaign is rigged. The brand has already shortlisted semi-known Instagram influencers for the roles. This audition is a mere formality—a common practice for the industry to show inclusivity. If only he could tell her . . . but he can't, because his salary depends on him feigning ignorance. Other than congratulating her on the take and telling her they'll get back to her soon, he can offer her no reassurance.

Meera walks out, beaming with satisfaction. A good performance always brings the sun out from behind the clouds. She walks past a billboard and imagines her face on it. If that were to happen, it would put to rest all the anxiety she had gone through when handing in her resignation.

Patti had supported her decision even as she narrated a harrowing tale from her younger years— of being propositioned by a magazine photographer when she was in a sari shoot. 'He looked at me with such lechery, it made me want to hit him below the belt! Times may have changed, chellam,[2] *but not that much. Promise me you'll watch out for yourself.'*

Raghu, as expected, had been displeased with her decision and complained. 'But you shot an ad just two months ago. You can't say your agency isn't bringing you offers. Plus, you have a steady income from the job here.' When Meera had told him she wanted to explore her prospects in Mumbai, he threw his hands up in the air. 'You have all your life to do that. Why now?'

---

[2] Term of endearment in Tamil; darling.

His tantrum had only increased her feelings for him. In fact, she was wildly turned on. No one had ever fought for her time or showered her with as much attention as he had. His passionate longing for her, though laced with possessiveness, was irresistible. This would soon be a memory they would laugh over. It would only be a matter of days before she received an affirmative callback and all would be glorious, just the way she had imagined.

She looks for the numbers on the list of local talent agencies that an acquaintance had given her. Surely, she has nothing to lose by shopping for agencies over the next few days. Hopefully, she will find a contract good enough to terminate the one she has with the Chennai agency. That would put a stop to the free run they've been having at her expense, charging a 20 per cent commission on her fee. She'd show them she could do better.

Meera begins contacting the agencies on her checklist, hoping each day would be like today, a silent affirmation of her decision.

'Have you modelled for fashion designers? We only invest our time in campaign shoots. You have the makings of a supermodel, which is why we're talking now. We are finicky about building our roster. We recently sent our models for the HoneyCave Cosmetics shoot to Dubai. We will charge a 30 per cent commission on all your projects. We are expensive only because we are effective. We will negotiate the right amount for you. Believe me, you will have so much work, you'll have to decline some of it! Our contracts . . .'

30 per cent! Did they say 30 per cent commission? The enthusiasm that had fuelled her agency hunt wanes a little. She hadn't foreseen agencies making lofty pitches with watertight contracts. *What else has she overlooked in her decision to move to Mumbai?* She must stop overthinking her choices. Tomorrow will be better. Besides, there are plenty of agencies out there. She needs to be patient. It takes time to find a match.

'We have a fabulous track record—99 per cent success rate. What about the 1 per cent? Sometimes, artists back out themselves, get married, quit working, dishonour the contract, etc.' The agent rattles off the names of famous clients he claims to have represented, but Meera isn't familiar with any of them.

'I formerly headed the reputed Swan agency. When I left, many of my models followed me here. We have a big shoot coming up in South Africa. They are looking for a face like yours. We don't chase models or actors. After all, it is our name on the line. I'm sure you want to go to South Africa. Who wouldn't want to travel internationally?'

Meera manages a polite smile as she grits her teeth at the agent's hubris.

She looks around the buzzing cafeteria grimly as her coffee cools on the table. It has all been a bit much to digest. Perhaps it'd be best if she held off on signing up with anyone new. At least she has her campaign callback to look forward to. Hopefully, that will come through and then she'll have the talent agencies eating out of her hands.

* * *

The sun is blazing in her room as Meera checks her phone groggily. She can't believe it's 2 p.m.! The last few days have been heavy; she had stayed awake most of last night. Even now, she wants to go back under the covers. She wills herself out of bed, knowing that strong coffee and a cold shower will fix how she feels.

Her phone beeps just then, showing a message from the casting supervisor:

> Hi Meera, thanks for your audition. Unfortunately, you weren't chosen. We will get in touch with you for future projects.

She sits on her bed, reading the message repeatedly. The coffee and shower can wait. She slumps back into bed, her childhood anxiety tugging at her, although this time, it's not because Appa is deaf to her wails, doggedly tearing her away from Patti, taking her to Bangalore (now Bengaluru). It's because she is starting anew in a strange city yet again and doesn't know where to begin. *What does she need to do to escape this anxiety?*

What was she thinking anyway? She's better off in Chennai, with a salaried job and breadcrumb acting roles. *Pack up, Meera! Go home.*

Take #2

From the Top

2012 B.C., Mumbai

'My name is Digambar Prasad Yadav. My height–'

'Are you related to Lalu Prasad Yadav, by any chance?' a young casting assistant asked, tongue firmly in cheek. The railways must limit the number of seats they allot to aspiring actors bound for Mumbai, he thought. He pushed aside the memory of his own overnight bus ride three years ago. Dozens like this boy came to Mayur Casting Studio expecting breakthroughs.

'No. I am from Bihar, from a small village in west Champaran jilla,[3] where the great Manoj Bajpayee sir comes from. My full name is Digambar Prasad Yadav, but everyone calls me Dabloo.'

---

[3] Zilla; a district that has its own local government.

'What's your height?' the assistant asked while replying to a message on his phone.

'5 feet 6 inches.'

He waved his hand at Dabloo who waved back and looked puzzled.

'That means you should show your left and right profiles, buddy. Hurry up!' The cameraman poked his head from behind the camera.

Dabloo turned sideways. These introductions before auditions were punishing. Why couldn't they jump straight into the performance and be done with it?

'I'm explaining this to you one more time, Raju!'

'Dabloo, sir.'

'After your name, height, home town and profiles, you have to tell us a little about yourself. We don't have all day!'

'Ye-yes, sorry. Like Manoj Bajpayee sir, I also belong to a farming family. My elder brother, Bindu bhaiya, runs his own business. He sells fertilizers, farming tools and equipment. He lives nearby, in Bettiah. Baba wanted me to complete my studies and join him on the farm, but bhaiya had other plans.'

'Okay, that's enough. We asked for a brief introduction, not your family history. We aren't making a biopic on you!' The casting assistant's remark gave vent to sniggers among the crew.

Mumbai had filled Dabloo with a mix of awe and apprehension—as if he were on a movie set watching an incredible bike stunt while running the risk of being hit. An audition followed another audition, some more *disastrous than others. The staff manning the gates of the casting studios would often look him up and down, and reject him as 'not fit'.*

He kicked at a stone as he walked past the glass walls of a gym. A large board above the entrance showed a muscular model posing with a dumb-bell beside the name Metal Fitness printed in bold letters. A muscular young man he recognized from one of the auditions was pulling and releasing an iron bar attached to a machine. They exchanged a fleeting look through the glass. Dabloo turned away. Should he enrol in a gym? The gym fee would cost him a kidney when he was barely making rent.

A seagull's squawks pulled his attention skyward— the bird flew across a palm tree, swooping down towards the ocean. It was a regular evening on Versova beach, with people jogging, playing volleyball and merrymaking. What stopped him from doing stretches and push-ups on the shore between auditions? The sea breeze hit him as he moved closer with a spring in his step.

* * *

The wind carries the perfume of nostalgia. Meera takes another bite-sized idli from the box and dips it into the coconut chutney before popping it into her mouth. The aroma of curry leaves makes her nose tingle. She couldn't have been more grateful for this sudden trip to Chennai to act in a mini web series. The timing was perfect—just when she was getting homesick amid the endless auditions in Mumbai and the subsequent waiting to hear back on the results (most of which were rejections).

'Patti is the best cook on the planet. How I missed her delicacies in Mumbai!'

'That's why I put off applying lipstick to the end, or you'd eat that too!' the make-up artist chuckles as he sweeps eyeshadow over her lids.

'I'm telling you, Niku, if Revlon makes lipsticks in Patti's home-made banana chips flavour, I'll eat their entire stock.' Meera grins, a mustard seed visible between her teeth.

'That good, is she? If I were you, I wouldn't wait to come to Chennai for a shoot; I would just pack Patti in a suitcase and take her with me to Mumbai. Because honestly, food in Mumbai tastes like a compromise.'

'I second that. Although, it's just been three months for me. I'm told my taste buds will come around eventually.'

'When is eventually? I've been in Mumbai for over six years now and nothing of that sort has happened to me.'

'Where are you from?'

'Kolkata, and I wait desperately for my annual holiday. Unless I get lucky and travel there for a shoot, just like you right now. Look at you, chomping away on home food and making me homesick.'

He steps back to balance the colour on Meera's other cheek.

'Here, you can have as many idlis as you like. I can always go home and eat more!' She offers him the insulated box.

'No, no, you keep the idlis. Just give me Patti,' he chuckles. 'But seriously, if you miss home food in Mumbai and want to try some Bengali delicacies, you should come over to my place. My partner makes the best shukto, and when he's in the mood, even breakfast is a feast!' He winks at the last part before breaking into a nasal laugh.

The production team, including the make-up artists, have been flown in from Mumbai. Niku's over-familiarity is puzzling. Was he as unrestrained before entering showbiz or is it a trait he's acquired over the years? He has already offered to connect her to important people in the industry. She knows many projects in Bollywood work because of the right friendships, but does she *have* to humour them to win favour?

'In fact, I'm hosting a dinner next month. Why don't you come over? Some of my industry friends will be there too, and thank God, they aren't your typical Bollywood folks, or we would never get along. Frankly, the only over-the-top (OTT) I can stand is the platform, never the people!'

'I don't know if that's going to be possible,' Meera says.

'Why not? Are you travelling?'

'No, I might be moving back to Chennai.'

'Already? Why? Isn't Mumbai where all the action is?'

'It's so difficult to find work without an agency,' she says as she fidgets with a box of hairpins. 'If I find a good one here, I can have both work and home food,' she says, tapping her feet on the footrest.

Niku knits his brows. *What is with these new actors giving up after facing a minor setback?* He picks up a contour stick. 'You've been in Mumbai for only three months. What were you expecting? And even in that short time, you've landed a small role in this web series.'

'Aram Nagar is an ocean of auditions! It's overwhelming!' she complains.

'That's good. Keep still.'

A few minutes later, he asks, 'Did you find this role through an agency or an audition call?'

'Audition call.'

'There you go! More than an agency, what you need is loads of perseverance. It took me five years to land my first feature film, and that too, only as an assistant make-up artist. That's when I started getting more work as an independent artist in commercials, web series and music videos. Agencies work only after you've earned a few credited roles; they merely fulfil the roles of managers. If you have no work, what are they going to manage? Just take Patti to Mumbai with you and audition your ass off!'

The next minute, he's gossiping about the costume department. Meera is grateful for the change of subject. The second most annoying thing after over-familiarity is how many people dispense unsolicited advice. But as she looks into the mirror, she thinks of what he said. If there is anyone she'd like to take with her to Mumbai, it is Raghu, but he insists on staying in Chennai. Perhaps she should make another attempt to convince him.

* * *

'Scene 5 Take 2.' The clapper boy slaps the slate together and runs out of the frame.

It's a ballroom setting. At the sound of 'Action!', a server holding a tray of glasses containing apple juice crosses the frame as the camera snakes through a crowd of smiling guests dressed in silks and jewels, and closes in on a couple slow dancing together. 'Cut!'

The director strides towards the cameraman for a conversation. Make-up and hair assistants pull out lip gloss, puffs and tail combs to apply retouches to the actors, while spot boys walk around the room holding paper cups and cans of water. Half an hour later, the crew swarming the director and the cameraman take note of the instructions for the next shot and disperse. The lighting technicians shift equipment across the room, the sound engineer is at his console wearing giant headphones, while the assistant directors scuttle around with scripts and walkie-talkies looking the worse for wear because of the gruelling schedule of the past week.

Meera looks at her script one more time before getting up for her shot. She spends the rest of the day playing out the scene from various angles.

In the middle of her last shot for the day, she catches a glimpse of a tall, square figure. Two deep-set eyes solemnly meet hers, making her heart flutter. It reminds her of that stunning scene from *Dirty Dancing*, where Johnny steps out of the wings into the spotlight and both he and Baby 'have the time of their lives'.

Meera averts her gaze to look at her co-actor whose lips seem to be moving inaudibly. Her body might be in the frame of the camera, but her mind is on the man in the shadows.

A thousand invisible strings bind her to him. From the moment she first met him, it was as if the men she'd dated before were mere distractions. Regardless of his entry into her life, which coincided with her mourning a recent heartbreak, he was no rebound. Truth is, no one else had evoked in her the kind of passion and attachment she felt towards him. It's unreal that even past their honeymoon phase, she should feel this helpless at the mere sight of him. Seven months of dating, followed by three months of staying apart and almost a year of knowing him! Yet when he waves at her now, she blushes to the roots of her hair. She recalls how he didn't leave her side from the time their eyes first met at the office party. Every spare moment of her life thereafter had been filled with his larger-than-life presence—the texting, the long drives, the movie dates and meals, the phone calls that lasted hours. She didn't care if her circle of friends had shrunk considerably. Raghu was her world.

And here he is, making her knees wobble like jelly.

'Cut! Meera, this is a close-up, so we don't have any margin for movement. Keep steady and up the intensity. You look distracted. I want to see in your eyes that you will kiss him, except that you don't. Just make me believe so,' the director says, clapping to alert the crew to prepare for another take.

The make-up assistant comes up to add more rouge but leaves without applying any. Meera's cheeks are red enough.

She centres herself, lets out a deep breath and focuses on the task at hand. As the action begins, she opens her eyes to meet her co-actor's, imagining for a few blissful minutes that he is Raghu.

'Cut! You really got me there, Meera.' Another look at the monitor, a nod from the sound team, and the director orders them to pack up. The director's appreciation and Raghu's surprise visit to the studio add a spring to her step.

* * *

'Not fit!' A casting intern holding fort at the studio's gates looked away from Dabloo and at the crowd of actors jostling to get in.

'It doesn't make sense! This character is a student. How much more fit do I need to look for the part?' Dabloo felt his jaw tighten. He had spent the last three and a half weeks training at Versova Beach. His upper arms felt firm and even appeared a little defined.

But he looked scrawny compared to the bulked-up actors beside him.

'The production is looking for upmarket actors–'

'What does that mean?' He spoke over the noise of the crowd.

'It means the actor has to look urban and speak fluent English.' She continued screening the actors, letting some pass through while dismissing the others.

How did she make an assumption about his English before even talking to him? He stomped out, vowing to learn the language. The goalposts just kept shifting!

'Over here, actors need to be thick-skinned. Don't let workshop instructors or wishy-washy interviews of celebs fool you. I'm the more experienced aspiring actor so I'm telling you like a brother,' Yogendra spoke between sips of his chai. He was one of the nine flatmates that Dabloo lived with in the two-room kitchen in Versova village.

'Take lessons online from YouTube. That's how I learnt the language, and now many people ask how I know such good English.'

Dabloo welcomed all the advice he got about how to find a foothold in the industry. It took him only a nudge here and a query there to get them talking about themselves. He followed up his YouTube lessons in grammar and pronunciation by practising reading aloud from stray newspaper pages, hoardings and instructions printed on cartons containing film equipment, apart from talking to Yogendra in Hinglish.

Yet, at the sound of 'Action', his facial muscles froze, his limbs disobeyed his mind and he fumbled over his dialogues.

'Clearly, he is not a Karmesh boy,' an auditioning supervisor said, referring to the A-list production house, Karmesh Films.

Dabloo wished he hadn't overheard those words.

'Let Karmesh films pick actors with "that sex appeal and South Bombay accent", what's holding you back from finding your own niche?' Yogendra said.

This remark consoled Dabloo a little. After all, Manoj Bajpayee sir must have also refused to give up when he was a newcomer, so why should he?

* * *

'For goodness' sake, Raghu, what is stopping you from finding a job in Mumbai?'

'We've already talked about this. You know I can't do that.'

'Can't or won't?'

'Same thing.'

Meera puts down her fork, glaring at him. She should have had this discussion after dinner because now she has lost her appetite.

'Why are you giving me that piercing stare?'

'I'm waiting for you to explain yourself. You know that I intend to build a career in the Hindi film industry, which, like it or not, is headquartered in Mumbai. Besides, the last time we had this conversation, you promised you would consider moving in with me.'

He looks sheepish. 'I said that because I didn't think you would actually make the shift. I thought you'd bask in your audition adventures for that deodorant or soap brand, get bored and return within a week. I'm surprised you even pulled off three months.'

'I intend to spend years in Mumbai,' she declares, taking large swigs of her wine.

Raghu reaches across the table to hold her hands. 'Baby, I didn't mean that. You know how much I've missed you. I'm just overwhelmed.' He placates her while gently massaging her fingers.

'I'm happy because you're here with me and sad that you want to leave soon. I thought we were going to spend our lives with each other. You know, get married, travel the world, open our own cafe, own a vacation home in the hills somewhere, make babies. Until you announced your movie plans out of the blue. You took me by surprise.' His voice cracks, endearing him even more to her. 'We are soulmates. I knew it from the day I first set eyes on you. You may not realize it now, but I love you even more than you love yourself. And I know that you want me too.'

She can't tell if it's the wine kicking in or Raghu's declarations of love that relax her into submission. She needs to gather her thoughts, so she looks away.

'What are you thinking, my precious?' he whispers.

'An assistant director on the shoot told me that my character might gain prominence in the show's second season. My acting gigs aren't a whim. It's perhaps the first time I have felt this strongly about—'

'Of course, it's not a whim. I saw you today and you were phenomenal! But I did feel like crushing your co-actor's bones.' He clenches his jaws while also pulling the bill away from Meera. He hands his card to the waiter.

'You can do your gigs from Chennai or travel for a project, if necessary. I think all you need is a good agency here with a pan-India network. I can speak with Shankar. His sister is a model and doing pretty well for herself. You should go meet her sometime. She'll give you good advice.'

Meera watches Raghu examine the bill closely before putting an illegible signature on it. She had never noticed how ugly and uneven his handwriting was—like that of a child learning his alphabet. As he puts the pen back into the folder, she feels a sudden rush of hormones. She wants him wrapped around her this very minute. Even though it's been a tiring day at work, her lust for him overpowers her need for rest. As he meets her eyes, he sees her desire in them.

'Shall we?' He offers her his arm as they leave the restaurant.

Take #3

Chennai Express

Muffled squeals of laughter spill out from the closed windows of the parked car, travelling four floors up and across Patti's balcony. For once, she isn't pleased about her hearing aid working well. She plucks it out of her ear, holding it tightly in her fist.

'I haven't seen you properly in five straight days, and you'll leave for Mumbai in another two!' Patti says as soon as Meera staggers in. 'Don't miss me when I'm dead and gone then.' She plugs her hearing aid back in.

'*Aiyo*,[4] Patti! Why would you say that? Once my shoot wrapped up, I went to Raghu's office party. I met some of my former colleagues too. Why is that an issue?' she groans.

---

[4] Exclamation to express distress, regret and grief.

'That boy is no good. Haven't you already told him that lack of sleep shows on camera the next day? And you know that alcohol makes your skin break out, but look at yourself! You're unable to walk straight!'

'Today was the last day of my shoot, so there's no question of eye bags or breakouts showing on camera. Besides, I'm all yours from tomorrow so stop being angry at me.' She grimaces as she hits her knee against the side table.

'Sure, you'll be home and sleeping all day,' Patti reaches for the jug of water, 'until that boy honks his car again, and you'll go flying out that door like before.'

Meera registers Patti's words a few seconds later and stops sharply.

'First, that was when we worked in the same office and he occasionally picked me up when I was running late. Second, I'm an adult. Why are you questioning my choices all of a sudden?'

'You have your entire life to make bad choices, but so long as I'm alive, I might as well drive some sense into you—'

'Which is?' Meera raises her eyebrows.

Patti exhales loudly and hands her a glass of water. 'I knew you excelled in dramatics at school, but I never thought you'd go for a career in the movies. Still, I was overjoyed when you chose to move to Mumbai. Yes, I was worried about your well-being, but thrilled nonetheless.'

Meera knows this is typical of Patti. She'd have some long-drawn-out point to make, ending by asking her to leave 'that boy' Raghu.

'You are an adult, and I don't want to come in the way of how you live your life, but you are still my little girl—who has been blinded by the promises of some boy she barely knew before falling madly in love with him.'

'What's wrong with that? Love is an instinct; it doesn't have to take years to recognize one's soulmate. And it's not like Raghu is some passing affair. We are quite serious about marriage.'

'True, but my fear is that your instincts have been hijacked, chellam. I don't know how and why, but—'

'But what?' Meera flails her arms wide, then drops them suddenly.

Patti pulls out a dining chair to sit on. 'It pains me to see you repeat your Appa's mistakes, Meera . . . He left your Amma for that other woman, and on her insistence—'

'Patti—'

'I haven't finished,' Patti speaks firmly. 'Not only did Vinod move to Bangalore, he did not even attend your Amma's cremation. Your face was red from crying when he came a year later to take you to Bangalore with him. You might not remember because you were too little.'

On the contrary, Meera wishes she could forget everything that followed Amma's death. *The sight of cotton being plugged into Amma's nostrils before an older cousin carried her to another room and handed her a colouring book and pencils to distract her. Even though she was only four, she knew Amma wasn't 'just taking a nap', as her cousin had suggested.*

Patti soon took on the role of her Amma and Appa. She avoided talking about both of them—to the extent that she would dodge the questions that Meera sometimes asked, by regaling her with one story or another (mostly those involving devas and asuras).[5] The one about Raktabeej fascinated Meera the most—the asura that duplicated himself with each drop of blood that fell to the ground when he was slayed by Goddess Kali. The stories helped to build her imagination and began to replace her thoughts of her parents. But a year later, Appa unexpectedly strode in, demanding that Meera go with him; the louder Meera cried the stronger Appa's grip became. In the years hence, she came to despise him, much like the asuras from the legends.

'Each of the thousand times you've told me about this incident, Patti, I've asked you the same question: Why did you let me go?'

'I was helpless! How could I fight your father for your custody? But it was a different story years later, when as a thirteen-year-old, you insisted on seeing me. You already know what happened next, but I'll still say it. He disowned you, his own child! And broke ties with me, his own Amma! Do you think he made all those decisions alone? Of course not! It was that scheming second wife of his. That's why it's so important to have your head firmly in place, especially when choosing a life partner.'

'Patti, I get that you don't approve of Raghu but stop making my situation akin to Appa's. He betrayed

---

[5] Gods and demons.

you, Amma and all of us. As for me, I'm not abandoning you. On the contrary, I am returning home.'

'All I'm saying is . . . *what*?' Patti adjusts her hearing aid.

'I intend to move back to Chennai. I'll travel for work when it comes, and stay with you, get to know Raghu better, just like you say, and . . .' Meera's reassurance tapers off.

'What happened to "Mumbai is the centre of auditions and films and opportunities"?'

'The city is overcrowded; too many people vying for the same job. All I need is a good agency here with a pan-India network.'

Whose words were these? She's such a far cry from the joyful girl she was just a year ago. Has a rakshasa[6] *taken possession of her senses?* Patti watches Meera stumble across the hallway towards her bedroom. She pulls out her hearing aid, wishing it could mute the voices in her head too: another partner scheming to separate her from her family.

At some point during the night, sleepless and wanting to escape the noise in her head, Patti puts on a recording of her all-time favourite soap opera. *The Bold and the Beautiful* plays on mute, the light from the screen dancing in her deep brown eyes.

Her life has been no less than a soap opera, what with adultery, alcoholism and death running through it. She lifts the photo frame of her late husband and

---

[6] Demon.

wipes it with her *pallu*.[7] Had he been alive, he would have helped raise their sons so differently, especially Vinod. He would never have let Vinod near a drop of alcohol, let alone allow him to spiral into alcoholism. He would have dealt with it with an iron hand, in a way that only Appas can. Is Meera suffering the same fate as her Appa? Is she turning to alcohol like him too? No, no, she's a disciplined girl, even more so because she couldn't bear the sight of Vinod drinking. It's only on this trip that she has indulged in some social drinking. But what about those few episodes during her corporate tenure? Is Raghu becoming Meera's alibi? What if Meera really is trying to numb her pain when she's with him, without knowing it? Patti holds her head between her hands.

* * *

'This rasam is delicious,' Raghu licks his fingers. 'I can't believe Patti invited me to lunch. Do you think she wants to talk to us about our future?'

'More like our present,' Meera says. Her plate of food remains untouched. She wonders what Patti intends to serve her guest—a polite sounding off, a nugget of wisdom or her blessings. Having spent decades teaching, Patti knew enough tricks to deal with all kinds of students. Certainly, this meal was merely an excuse and Patti hadn't shared her real

---

[7] A Hindi word commonly used to refer to the loose end of a sari or dupatta that is draped over the shoulder.

reason for inviting Raghu, no matter how much Meera had prodded. 'She was concerned about my moving back to Chennai, but I guess she has made peace with the idea of our being together after all.'

'Shouldn't your being here make her happy?' he asks.

'Oh, I'm thrilled about it!' Patti bustles in with more appam, thwarting further conversation. 'At least I can monitor her diet and rest, possibly even her schedule. You know how actors have managers? I could be hers if she lets me.'

Meera busies herself making balls of rice and rasam, arranging them on her plate without actually eating any.

'That aside, Meera told me that a friend of yours could help her sign up with an agency. Tell me, Raghu, would your friend also know an agency that would sign older people like me? I could really use my retirement to pursue my interests, in addition to being her manager, of course. Who knows, we could be the new granny–granddaughter duo in town!'

The second hand on the clock ticks loudly as Raghu fumbles before coming up with a vague response.

'I acted in a few stage plays in my younger days, but after Meera's grandfather's passing, I had to fend for the family. It left me with no time for myself. Now I hope to wet my toes in the modelling and acting industry. It is quite unnerving to be a newcomer, so maybe your friend could handhold both of us.' She chuckles with delight and a pink tinge on her cheeks.

Meera eyes Raghu—his broad, masculine shoulders droop as if weighed down by the lightness of Patti's being.

Meera's phone rings—she steps aside to answer it and comes back grinning like a Cheshire cat.

'That was from the casting office,' she says. They've cast me for a short film called *The Zombie*.'

'That's wonderful news, chellam! I knew you had it in you. If only you'll give it more of your time,' Patti says, smiling. 'When does shooting begin?'

'Next week, somewhere on the outskirts of Mumbai. Now, I'll have to stay a while longer in Mumbai until the shoot wraps up.'

Patti sees Raghu's face change colour. *What is it about him that repels her so much?*

'Congratulations!' His smile seems forced. 'Beware of hoax callers though; girls like you are easy targets,' he warns.

The disapproval underlying his tone does not escape Patti, and this time, it does not escape Meera either.

'This is a known casting agency; there shouldn't be any trouble,' Meera says. Involuntarily, she exchanges a look with Patti. *Girls like you? What does he mean?* She's determined to give him an earful when they are alone.

Clueless about their wordless interaction, Raghu adds, 'Shankar's sister has set up a meeting for you with an agency next week. She has really gone the extra mile to swing this, and now you're saying you won't be here. Consider what you are giving up for some short film.'

That night, Meera pulls out the diary bound in tan leather and ragged at the edges. She runs her fingers over the name embossed in peeling gold letters: *Revathi*. The paper inside is brittle and smells musty but the handwriting is clear. This is Amma's log of her poems and short stories—Meera's most prized possession because she feels it embodies Amma's soul. It is the first thing she would save in a fire, along with the sepia photograph from her first birthday which serves as a bookmark in the diary.

She turns the pages, asking herself the same question she asks each time she opens the diary. *Why did Amma never publish this? Why are the last several pages blank, as if she discontinued writing midway?* Meera knew the answer to her questions. Appa's frequent discouragement of Amma's writings had eventually poured cold water over her ambitions.

Raghu's attitude from earlier had left her unsettled. *Was she in love with a younger form of Appa?*

Take #5

The Auditionees

If struggle and hardship were to be seen as ammunition, then the past eight years have made Dabloo a weapon of mass destruction—who continues to amass ammunition with hundreds more auditions in Mumbai along with small commercial stints that come his way every now and then. Once the hesitant migrant, Dabloo now moves with the confidence of a Mumbaikar. The 'fake it till you make it' advice he got from one of his co-actors has become his mantra.

'They shut up when I told them our Dabloo has been cast in thirty-four TV commercials and twenty-two feature films,' Bindu bhaiya's proud voice crackles through the phone.

'Bhaiya, I was cast in the feature films mostly as a crowd artist or a small role. It is no big deal; you should have let them think whatever they want to,' Dabloo says.

'How could I let it go? You took a brave step in the direction of your dreams and proved us all wrong. Your no smoking public service awareness (PSA) film still plays in the cinema hall, and each time you appear on screen, the whole hall starts whistling and clapping. They cheer louder for you than for the movie's hero. So, what's wrong if I told Shakuntala bhabhi to go to the cinema hall before making remarks about your career?'

The PSA for no smoking had turned out to be Dabloo's very first acting assignment in Mumbai after he was rejected for an audition for a feature film. Nonetheless, the rejection hadn't dimmed his enthusiasm for being on an ad film set, and donning hospital scrubs for a costume with prosthetic ulcers applied near his mouth (so long as he did not look at himself in the mirror).

At lunch, a junior artist sat across from Dabloo and remarked on his audacity.

Dabloo didn't understand what he meant.

'Taking this role is a huge risk. The PSA is being made to look like a testimonial from life. It's so easy to get typecasted in this industry. You could easily become that dead man from the no smoking campaign that no one would want to recognize as alive.'

Dabloo's face fell as the man continued. 'Don't worry, brother, the good news is that public memory is very short. The only way to make people forget a role is to keep playing as many different ones as you can.'

'Bhaiya, I have to go now or I'll be late for the set.'
He ends the call before Bindu bhaiya can ask for details.
Bhaiya would be crestfallen if he knew that his kid
brother was a cable operator on the film's unit, not an
actor. It's not his first stint to supplement his income—he
has hustled several odd jobs as a camera assistant, spot
boy, watchman, waiter, mime artist and snack server at
cinema halls. Bhaiya is so easily overcome by emotion.
Had he known, he would definitely have sent Dabloo
money and that would have been a blow to his dignity.
God forbid, if things become dire, he'd rather be broke
than take money from bhaiya.

Maybe some day, when he is successful, he will
be able to look back with pride at the by-lanes and
dirt alleys he's had to travel. But if he doesn't leave
right now, he'll be terribly late; one can never tell with
Mumbai's traffic.

Dabloo sprints down the steps and on to the street,
hailing an auto bouncing over potholes. 'Andheri station!'

* * *

Meera holds up her fifth whiteboard of the day. It reads:

Name:	Meera Kanthan
Age:	27
Height:	5'8"
Competitive brands:	No
Available on shoot dates:	Yes
Reference:	Direct

She's auditioning for a supermarket commercial. The scene shows her playing cards with her friends and drawing a lucky hand.

'Win big at the grand Diwali bonanza. Massive discounts and exciting gifts. Only at the Grand Grocers!' she says with a wide grin.

The casting supervisor throws out instructions, trying to be heard over the swelling crowd of actors in the makeshift waiting area. It is one of those chicken factory auditions that are commonplace in Mumbai. Most production houses and studios operate from temporary structures and spaces on hire because real estate is so expensive.

'You have drawn three aces. Amplify the excitement and improvise more on the friendly banter. Silence everybody, and . . . Action!'

During the shot, someone's phone in the crowd begins to ring. The supervisor shrieks, making the cameraman almost lose his grip on the equipment. 'Quiet! This is an audition room, not your living room! I want the extra people out of the room now!'

Meera and her screen-friends' excitement wanes for the next two takes, and after their final take, they are dismissed bluntly. But it doesn't matter because there's a mob of actors awaiting their turn. The casting team will have enough 'options' to share with the production house.

As she walks out, she runs into Divya. 'Can you believe it? She cut us off right in the middle of the take to scream at the crowd?! If she's so frustrated with her job, why is she still doing it?' Meera fumes.

'Moolah!' Divya says with a twinkle in her eyes. 'Look around you. This is Aram *Nagariya*[8]—a melting pot of casting offices and production houses. It may look like brick huts with straw roofs, but if you've been around long enough, you know that some seriously influential decisions are taken behind those doors. There are more than enough people vying for a project, probably the supervisor as well. For all you know, she is preserving her job at the cost of her sanity.'

'You think?'

'Absolutely! I get her angst. This is a maddening place to be in 24/7, and the TV commercials are the worst of all. As for actors, giving up a precious half-day to audition for thirty-second commercials and hoping to get visibility for film offers? Exhausting. That's why I've decided to stick to the stage,' Divya flicks the last of her cigarette away. 'TV commercials are an adulterous pursuit. If you are a true artist, the stage is where you should be.'

'What about paying one's rent? Surely the stage alone cannot provide that.'

'There's plenty of work in the arts outside commercial cinema. Backstage production, playwriting, workshops or other creative projects that one can work on solo or in collaboration. It won't make you rich, but it'll take care of the bills. To be honest, I always find myself questioning artists who haven't suffered enough for their art.'

---

[8] A casual way of saying 'Nagar' meaning a town, a city, an area in a city or a suburb.

Meera wonders if Divya has always had the starving artist syndrome or if she's just bitter about prematurely giving up commercial cinema and TV.

'Which play are you rehearsing?'

'Do you know the award-winning playwright, Anuradha Mittal? She's making her debut as a director. The play is centred on a social activist's fight against the oppressive system. We are doing a showcase on the tenth of next month, followed by ticketed shows across major metropolitan cities.' She goes on to talk about another project, her now-on-now-off relationship and her three-legged rescue cat until she breaks off to suggest getting a coffee.

'Yes! It's been a long day—first house-hunting, then auditions,' Meera says.

'When did you move out of that PG accommodation?'

'Two months ago. The building caught fire and burned to the ground.'

Divya gasps. 'Where are you staying now?'

'At a women's hostel in Powai.'

'That's quite far from here. I'll put you in touch with my broker. He knows a few places around this area.'

Some distance away from the cafe, Meera's sandal's strap gives way. 'Damn! I carried these to change into after I'm done with auditions. My heels will be ruined if I wear them on these unpaved roads of Aram Nagar.'

'So don't wear them,' comes Divya's pat response. 'Do you know, *nukkad natak*[9] artists perform barefoot

---

[9] Street theatre.

most of the time? Sometimes, taking off one's shoes is part of an actor's preparation for getting into the character's shoes.'

'I'm not a street play artist, but that's what I'll do, I guess—only because this character loves her favourite stilettos and doesn't want them ruined!' Meera pulls off her footwear and they walk towards a nearby coffee shop.

The newly opened Cafe Blue is charming, with its cane furniture and lime-green upholstery, and an equally delectable menu for coffee and all-day breakfast. But, it is the cafe's prime location overlooking the sea that has made it the haunt for Bollywood aspirants and hotshots alike.

'No tables available for another fifteen minutes,' the waiter says. 'Why don't you place your order in the meantime?'

'Will you order me a cappuccino, Meera? I'll make a quick trip to the ladies' room.' Divya enters the cafe, greeting acquaintances as she moves through.

While waiting near the outdoor seating area, Meera watches the last of the dipping sun. The sky looks splendid—as it did during that drive along the Pondicherry (now Puducherry) coast, that time when Raghu and she had gone on a weekend getaway. It had been a rough week at work, making her desperate for Friday evening to arrive soon. She had no grand plans for her birthday on Sunday, except that Patti would slice the freshly made Mysore Pak (Patti loved announcing plans in advance), after which they would probably catch a musical performance in town. Raghu had to travel to Hyderabad for a conference and wasn't expected back until next week. His call at dawn on Saturday had woken her up.

'How I long to be right beside you, when I hear that morning voice of yours,' Raghu said.

'Then come back soon.'

'Actually, why don't you just step out on to your balcony for a moment?'

It took her a few seconds to grasp what he was saying as she propped herself up against the pillows. 'What do you mean?'

She looked over the railing and there he was! Holding a bouquet of the brightest yellow lilies. She must have been gaping in disbelief long enough for him to ask her to hurry up, pack her bags and meet him downstairs.

Pressing the phone to her ear, she spoke in low, excited tones. 'Wait! What? 'Where are we going?'

His eyes bore into her as he said, 'You'll know soon. And don't forget your swimsuit.'

Meera was too caught up in the wave of excitement to ask him how he knew those were her favourite flowers because she didn't recall making any mention of it. They'd barely started to get to know each other, but being with Raghu was already feeling familiar. In fact, being with him felt like speed-reading a romance novel. She wondered what more surprises he had in store for her once they got to their destination.

Raghu had planned a birthday surprise for Meera in Pondicherry. What a delightful time they had! Their conversations were endless, punctuated only by pillow fights and lovemaking. The next day, when he brought her breakfast in bed, she planned her entire life with him. He proposed they seal the deal with a swim in the ocean. Raghu really knew the way to her heart.

What would life have been like, had the facewash audition not come along weeks later?

The thought erases the involuntary smile on her face. The anger she'd felt at his 'girls like you' comment disappears below the horizon with the sun. They had barely spoken in the past two months because of the fight his comment had caused. Afraid that he sounded like Appa, she had gone off on a tangent, accusing him of all the follies that plague men. Raghu was thrown off but maintained that he was just being protective of her.

This is something about herself that she hasn't understood. Why should a fight make her withdraw from him with little contact for weeks? It's as if she goes on putting hurtful events into a deep freezer to numb herself from the sting of pain. But it's different with Raghu. No matter what, she is unable to let her feelings for him frost over.

A pang of longing arises as she misses the hypnotic sound of his voice and his strong arms wrapped around her on her bad days. Above all, she misses his little tantrums and the fact that he makes it so easy for her to vent to him, even if she has had to repeat herself to be fully heard every now and then. Raghu confuses and comforts her all at once.

She must call him. She's aching to share the details of how difficult the last two months have been—with her apartment building burning down, a surge in auditions and the struggles of house-hunting.

'Ma'am, your table is ready,' the waiter says.

She turns around to look at him when she notices Mickey Taneja sitting at a neighbouring table, his face partially hidden by a dark baseball cap. Though it isn't unusual to spot known faces in this part of town or anywhere in Mumbai for that matter, it's rare to see one of the most sought-after casting directors in Bollywood in a busy cafe. All the eyes on him are looking away now and then, so they're not caught staring. It's just a matter of time before he begins to be hounded by desperate job- and role-seekers.

He is sitting with two women. One looks like a Barbie—her pearly white smile and alabaster skin glow in the evening light. The other is a middle-aged lady who looks pleased, nodding and speaking occasionally.

As she walks to her table, Meera looks at the Barbie lookalike resentfully. *She'd bag a film role very soon.* Just then, she misses her footing, and in trying to recover her balance and avoid stepping on the dog spreadeagled on the floor, she knocks a plate off Mickey's table.

The sound of crockery breaking draws everyone's attention to her. Red-faced, she mumbles an apology.

'Watch out for the glass shards. Oh! Where are your shoes?' Mickey looks back up at her.

She wipes her feet on the back of her jeans. 'My sandal strap broke on the way . . .'

Mickey's attention is drawn away as a waiter approaches to clean the mess.

Meera is pulling her heels out of her bag when Mickey and the two women push back their chairs to get up and leave. There's some talk about a meeting in the coming week, which makes the Barbie lookalike break into a broad smile.

Divya returns in time to find Meera watching the casting director drive off and asks, 'What happened here?'

'I might just have done an impression of myself. You know that moment when you're attempting a sashay but walk straight into a glass wall because you didn't see it?'

'If it makes you feel any better, Taneja is casting for Yashika Saini's next film which is based on the Indian women's cricket team. You could try getting in touch with his office. Maybe they are looking for actors with quirks!' Divya laughs as Meera straightens in her chair, ears pricked up.

It's incredible how in spite of pooh-poohing auditions and the depravity of Bollywood, Divya is always in the know. 'My friend knows the people at Taneja's office, and they want someone with an athletic physique. Email them your profile and I'll ask him to put in a word with the auditioning supervisor,' Divya says.

Take #6

Slipping a Mickey

At the Reels Conclave 2019, the emcee is spotlit against the backdrop. The event's name is printed in royal blue above its logo of a film reel morphing into a microphone. 'Ladies and gentlemen, the next person to take the stage has introduced some of Bollywood's most talented names, who've gone on to become India's biggest stars. If casting is an art, then he is the master artist. He is none other than Mickey Taneja!' The emcee's voice gives way to uproarious applause from the audience comprising models, actors, independent talent and casting agents.

A stout, bespectacled middle-aged man walks up the steps, acknowledging the applause with a namaste. He is felicitated by the organizers before being shown to a plush armchair bearing his place card. Placing it on the side table, he sits down, pushes up his spectacles, adjusts the microphone attached to the armrest and clears his throat. Unknown to the audience, he also clears his conscience.

The #MeToo allegation made against him two weeks ago has cast a shadow on his image. The organizers had agreed to still feature him as a speaker only because he was recommended by influential friends who continue to rally for him and protest his innocence.

'This public backlash on a few social media handles is a flash in the pan. The best way to counter them is to announce new projects and more casting calls,' a film-maker friend had said.

Anamika, the agent responsible for finalizing Mickey as the casting director for the prestigious American Studio Network's (ASN) new show, is chewing her fingernails. She's praying for Mickey to stick to the script—he had shredded the physical copy of his speech the night before, after a tiff with a member of the press who had written an article labelling him a womanizer and a bully. Mickey had even threatened to withdraw from today's event. It took significant cajoling on her part (and the listening skills of a saint) to calm him. Fanning the egos of important people is as much a part of her job description as is lobbying for their business projects.

The mic crackles as Mickey taps on it. 'The business of showbiz thrives on originality—whether it's an idea or an individual. Nowadays, even a decent imitation of the original is considered original.' He sees some members of the audience taking notes. 'No matter how talented an actor is, if their talent cannot be seen on camera, it's pointless. And then, there are many actors who, even with just passable talent, have gained public admiration. After three decades in the casting industry, I can identify who's in it for the joy of the craft and who's for the fanfare,' he says, snapping his fingers.

Meera sits in the audience, wondering what impression Mickey must have formed of her over a month ago at the cafe. She had emailed her profile for Yashika Saini's film the very next day but did not hear back. They must have finished casting. Or maybe the process has been delayed because of the allegation he's facing. Had he propositioned that Barbie lookalike too?

The woman who accused Mickey has not revealed her identity, nor has she filed an FIR (First Information Report). In fact, she's been reported missing. Has Mickey Taneja threatened her into silence? So much goes on behind closed doors; maybe it's a good thing she hasn't got the callback for an audition. Can't women see through hollow promises or crooked intentions? If it were her, she would hit the man below the belt, in Patti's words.

She notices the middle-aged woman (the one she saw at the cafe with Mickey) rise from her chair in the front row to greet two people. Ushers rush in with extra chairs for the grey-haired white man and his brunette companion. The man puts a stack of business cards in his pocket before sitting down. That must be how many potential business contacts he's already met at the convention.

Mickey's speech ends and the emcee opens the house to questions. A woman in her mid-sixties introduces herself as a member of the press. She asks him about the scandal, making all heads turn sharply towards her.

Even as the emcee lifts the mic to protest, Mickey responds. 'It's true that women in the entertainment industry face harassment, sexism and body shaming as you say, but there are also some cases of sour grapes. I'm not downplaying any of their experiences, but . . .'

'Sour grapes? Related to your indulging in sexual misconduct?' the journalist asks.

'That's jumping to a conclusion, ma'am,' the emcee says amid murmurs from the audience.

Anamika makes a ball out of her fist, opening it as she exhales. Mickey inhales deeply, pushes up his spectacles and clears his throat once again. 'It's possible that this accuser is acting out of frustration at being rejected for a role. The decision to sign an actor for a movie rests with the director or producer. I'm a casting director and my job is to find the most suitable artists for the roles and communicate that to the makers. No more, no less.'

'So, you know who she is?'

'No, ma'am, I don't know this woman. I said it's *possible* she's acting out of frustration. In fact, the police are trying to trace her. If she is a victim, why has she vanished within a week of making this accusation?'

The journalist is relentless, but this time, Mickey cuts her off mid-sentence by pointing to the next hand that shoots up. The emcee fidgets with his watch, throwing glances backstage as Mickey takes a few sips of water. Despite being as quick as they can, the ushers take agonizingly long to pass on the mic to the next audience member.

'Good afternoon, my name is Meera Kanthan and I'm an actor. I am from Chennai, but I now live in Mumbai. Mine is more of a dilemma than a question, but I'm sure some of the people in the audience will resonate with it. I find that I'm often typecast during auditions and by talent agencies because of my curly hair and city of origin. I may look the part, and even be as talented as anybody else in the room, yet I see mostly foreigners or Indians who look like they are international supermodels being pushed to the head of the queue or grabbing most of the primary roles. Does talent really matter, or should I start introducing myself as half-Spanish?'

The audience breaks into laughter and Mickey smiles as well.

'We primarily look for talent in an actor, and if the script demands a specific appearance, then that. Perhaps, you have not attended auditions at our office. To give credit where it's due, many casting offices now are pro—'

Her pulse throbs faster as she blurts, 'Didn't get the chance, sir. I sent my profile a month ago but did not get a callback.'

She should have shut up! How did it matter? It's not like he recalls their previous interaction, and even if he does, she was Miss Clumsy with grubby feet. But isn't any attention good attention? At least, now, he'll remember her as the girl with the (grubby) foot in her mouth!

Mickey scratches his goatee, eyeing her intently—perky breasts, full lips, tall, athletic build and dark eyes. She looks familiar. 'What did you say your name was?'

'Meera Kanthan.'

* * *

'Is this why they asked me to speak? So that they could have some crazy fake news lady explode all over me? It's even more embarrassing that Jerry and Carol of ASN were witness to this.' Mickey swallows his diabetes pill.

'I spoke to the coordinator at Reels. He is very sorry . . .'

'Sorry, my foot! Tell me honestly, Anamika, is there a conspiracy against me? Are you a part of it? I mean, look at the timing of it all. I sign a contract with ASN, and two days later, some anonymous woman throws a wild accusation at me. I almost back out as speaker but you convince me to attend, and I'm humiliated there. Even after instructing Reels to screen all audience questions.'

He has become increasingly petulant since the #MeToo allegation was made. In the months until then, Anamika had seen him as a man heady with success, but now he is a man losing the plot.

'That's enough! I'm not your manager or assistant at whom you can throw a tantrum. I only talked you into going ahead with the session out of goodwill. It would have been worse had you not attended. People would have assumed you're guilty and hiding. But now that you're down in the dumps, you want to chop off the hands that are trying to pull you up. So be it! I don't know about ASN, but I'm thinking of ending our agreement,' she says, folding her arms across her chest.

Mickey stops pacing and sits down. Her threat works, and he mumbles an apology before pressing the buzzer and calling for tea and snacks.

He asks, softly this time, 'Why did you invite Jerry and Carol to the event when we were to meet later this evening?'

'I did not! They called me during your speech saying they were at the event and had just found out that you were onstage. That's when I invited them in.'

'Who would have told them about the Reels Conclave?'

'Come on, Mickey! It's a global convention of the Indian film and media industry. You think they wouldn't have seen the ads? It's a meet-and-greet event for all kinds of media houses, casting and talent agencies, and marketing firms. These guys are television producers and are probably shopping for local collaborators for *B-Strugglers* or their other shows. Stop being a conspiracy theorist.'

Mickey drums his fingers on the desk, leaning back in his chair. *When ASN had approached him for their reality series centred on the lives of struggling actors in Bollywood, he hadn't been able to stop thinking about it. The show had all the ingredients of an international award winner, given Americans' fascination with the*

Slumdog Millionaire *impression of India. Global recognition would mean financiers and producers queueing up to back his other projects.*

His thoughts are interrupted by Anamika's phone. She looks at it and says, 'Jerry regrets he needs to cancel today's meeting. Carol and he are unwell. He'd like to postpone the meeting to the day after tomorrow.'

'Why not tomorrow?'

'I guess they are jet-lagged,' she says absently.

'Jet lag, my foot. For all you know, they are contacting other casting directors to identify a replacement for me.'

The office boy brings tea and snacks, placing a sachet of artificial sweetener next to Mickey. After he leaves, the silence in the room is palpable.

Mickey sees Anamika add three sugar cubes to her tea as opposed to the usual two. 'Something on your mind?' he asks. With no choice but to keep a strict vigil on his sugar intake for the past five years, Mickey has come to consider people's use of sugar as a reflection of their state of mind. Which has helped him negotiate some complicated business deals.

'It's my son. He's upset because I couldn't spend Diwali with him last month in Delhi. Now he insists that I show him my flight ticket for New Year's as proof! He has stopped believing me. The poor kid is already stressed because of the divorce. If I cancel again because of work, he'll never speak to me.'

'You do what you must, but we need to make *B-Strugglers* happen at all costs. This is my ticket to Hollywood.'

She looks at him—the bags under his eyes, his receding hairline, his lined forehead and his nose scrunched to keep his spectacles in place—and resolves to book her tickets even if the dates clash with meetings for Mickey's project.

'I'm sick of being typecast as that casting guy. I want to produce, maybe even direct films, and work with a set of people who don't know me, my language, my background or my past. I know it doesn't make sense coming from someone like me. But it's a pretty joyless ride with the same set of people and their hypocrisy and double-dealing.'

She sips her tea quietly. Mickey's recent mood swings have made her wonder if it's the pills he keeps popping or his midlife crisis rearing its head. Either way, his behaviour reinforces one truth about human nature. Fear of the past catching up often makes one take dangerous leaps of faith or makes them hysterical, like Mickey's being. Given his history of sexual harassment, perhaps this false accusation is karma at work.

The loss of face following the allegation and a possible falling out with ASN isn't just an irrational fear of Mickey's—she can see it coming too.

* * *

Meera presses the hot water bag to her stomach, hoping the pressure will ease her cramps. It's been an untimely period yet again—something that has been occurring since she discontinued the allopathic medicines for her polycystic ovary syndrome (PCOS). The side effects were making her skin break out too badly to be hidden, no matter how much concealer she applied.

Her rants had sent Patti on a mission—that of finding alternative remedies. She had tracked down an old student whose mother was an herbalist and couriered the medicines along with a dozen other supplements, oils and face packs. 'The pimples will dry and flake off within a day,' she'd said.

As for her legs, Meera wonders if it's the period or the intensive house-hunting of the last few weeks that's causing this bone-crushing ache. Maybe it's not worth her time to look for any more apartments—the ugliest one had blue and white tiles on the walls of the living room, while the other two had toilets smaller than Patti's Godrej almirah.

The apartment at Four Bungalows[10] is the only decent one, but the rent, broker's fee and security deposit are over her budget.

She groans as she massages her legs from calf to sole. If only she had a massage roller! Maybe another dose of those herbal pills might work? She pops one, then rubs oil on her stomach and legs. Warm and soothing, it lulls her to sleep.

She's falling off a tall building. As she nears the ground, what looked like ants earlier reveal themselves to be humans; shrubs grow into oak trees; tealights turn into lamp posts. She whizzes past windows of the multi-storey building, with a strange shadow hot on

---

[10] A colony in suburban Mumbai.

her tail, before she hits the ground. She has turned into a splotch of ketchup. Surprisingly, she doesn't feel any pain or remorse.

The phone startles her awake. She licks her dry lips and says hoarsely, 'Yes, I'm Meera Kanthan.' As the caller continues to speak, she drinks from her sipper, careful to make no sound. 'Yes, yes, I can come over tomorrow. Thank you.'

A current of excitement runs through her body. She's been invited to audition for Yashika Saini's cricket film! Just as instantly, she reminds herself that this is merely a call for the audition and that she hasn't been hired.

She jumps out of bed, spreads the sheet, sweeps the floor and takes a shower. Her aches and pains have vanished—those herbs are magic! Or is it the call for an audition that has worked? She's full of beans, a complete contrast to how she was feeling before her nap. Has she woken up into a dream?

She wiggles her toes impatiently while the audition script opens on her phone.

Meera gets gooseflesh as she reads Naintara's character sketch. Like her, Naintara too, is vulnerable to the pressures of a highly demanding profession, but she carries the responsibility of being the Indian women's cricket team captain with poise. Little does she know that the cricket board and sponsors are about to replace her for the upcoming miniseries with the less experienced niece of a board member.

Meera is devastated at how unceremoniously Naintara is shown the door, that too at an official party hosted for the Indian team. She bites her lip.

Is Naintara furious or collected? Does she walk out after slamming her glass on a table, or does she watch from the sidelines as the drama unfolds, vowing to herself that she will make a comeback?

Meera spends the evening memorizing lines before she assigns emotions and a metre to the words. Every dialogue is a loose wire, requiring her to pull them tight. Her first voice modulation is too dramatic, so she decides to try the tennis ball exercise she'd learned at a workshop. She aims a tennis ball at a point on the wall, uttering her dialogues in a neutral tone. On repeating her lines, she finds them sounding much more natural. But they still need fine-tuning. All she has to do is decide her body language and positioning. But her body feels stiff, as if the dialogues she's speaking mean nothing. *Even a voice actor in a sound studio is more physically expressive.* She exhales sharply and falls on to the bed.

'Go easy, Meera. At the worst, they'll tell you they'll get back and won't. Breathe. You can handle the rejection; you've done it enough times. Just handle the nerves.'

Meera remembers her movement class from the same workshop. She closes her eyes and lets her body take the lead—her arms move in waves and she's on her feet again, swirling, hair flying as she spins. She bends at the waist, making circles with her shoulders. She is beginning to find a rhythm to her movement, as if she's a stream aligning with the river of the story and of her character's life. Slowing to a stop, Meera sits on the floor to calm herself before she begins again.

This time, she embodies Naintara just right. It feels nothing short of magical!

* * *

The branches of trees sway outside the French window at Mickey Taneja's office, as the mid-December sunshine streams in. *Winter is the most pleasant season of the year in Mumbai*, Meera thinks. The weather makes her want to sit at an outdoor cafe with a book or a friend. If she can get this performance right, she will have hit it out of the park. No, she must not get ahead of herself. She must rein in her fantasies and focus on the audition. She gets back to pacing the corridor and committing her dialogues to memory.

'I'm Reshma. I head the casting team at MT Studio.'

Reshma's burgundy-tinted hair is arresting, and her hazel eyes and narrow chin make her look fierce. The thickly applied kohl is smudged over the crinkles on her skin while her smoker's lips are prominent beneath the peachy gloss. Making small talk, Reshma leads the way to a comfortable-sized room with wooden flooring, a table with a few chairs, studio lights, reflectors and a camera on a tripod.

'We'll do a rehearsal before we go into take,' Reshma says, signalling to the cameraman to begin rolling the camera. 'Are you ready to go, Naintara?'

Meera nods.

* * *

'Of course, I know how to ride a bike—I'm just out of practice,' Meera says while struggling to mount the Royal Enfield Thunderbird 350cc. She had to rely on Divya's friend to lend her a motorcycle.

Divya holds the sissy bar to keep it steady. 'That's why one must watch out when making tall claims at auditions. What if you actually get cast for your riding skills?'

'It was the trashiest audition ever, I promise you. I'm surprised they picked me,' Meera says.

'So, you're saying your acting was pathetic, and now they'll find out your biking skills are negligible. Why don't you decline the role and save face?'

'You must be joking! Five rounds of this field and I'll be good to go. Besides, I only have a small stretch to ride during the shoot. They'll be bringing in a stuntwoman for the racing part.'

'Maybe your resolution for 2020 should be to learn how to ride a bike well.'

Meera turns on the ignition and the motorcycle sputters to life. She gets off to a wobbly start before she finds balance and control. It's not as difficult as she'd thought it would be. In fact, she's almost beginning to enjoy the ride. She's on her fourth round when the phone rings. *It might be the stylist from the ad shoot, confirming details for the costume trials.*

Minutes later, Meera brakes the motorcycle inches away from Divya, who jumps back to avoid being run over, giving her a death stare. 'You look thrilled for someone with awful riding skills!'

'Tell me, could your friend lend me a cricket bat too? Because you are now looking at the captain of the Indian cricket team in Yashika Saini's feature film, *Bowled Over*.'

Take #7

The Stereotype

A cluster of well-dressed aspirants wait outside the Big Screen Glory office at Aram Nagar. The music reverberates through the walls. Jayesh sits in his air-conditioned car, waiting for Bidyut's green signal to go in.

Bidyut, who'd turned out to be co-founder of this casting agency, and he had bonded over workout sessions at the gym. So, when the opportunity of an online commercial came along, Jayesh was among the first to know. Bidyut had mentioned it in the middle of a weight-training session, and the news had made Jayesh lose his rep count.

A young boy, probably a helper or cleaner at the office, taps at his car window, asking him to proceed for the audition. Being friends with the casting director means that he doesn't have to be packed in the waiting room, like the other actors and dancers.

A lanky casting intern holding a clipboard steps forward to talk to the swelling crowd.

'This is an audition for the soon-to-be-launched Rhythm app. It's the Indian version of TikTok but with additional features like dance and music tutorials. The production is looking for an ensemble cast and a mash-up of dance genres. So, the house-help could be moonwalking, the office-goer could loosen his tie and break into Kuchipudi, an elderly lady could use her walking stick as a *nunchaku*,[11] etc., in tune with the music. You can get as creative as you like!'

Jayesh doesn't know any of those moves. 'Could I be the guy doing push-ups in a club?' he asks.

'You'd need to become a character, like a teacher, doctor or sportsman, and mix it with arm waves, head tilts or any other element of dance. But no twerking, please.' The intern jostles his way out of the waiting room, leaving the candidates to hustle for rehearsal space. A few of them step out on to the verandah.

Ever since he's amassed 10,000 fans on TikTok by making videos based on trending ones, Jayesh has let the internet do his thinking for him. There are no original ideas in this world anyway, so he might as well rehash an idea for the audition too. Just then, he gets

---

[11] The nunchaku is a traditional East-Asian martial arts weapon consisting of two sticks, connected to each other at their ends by a short metal chain or a rope.

a call from an unknown number. Thinking it could be from a casting agency, he steps away to answer it.

'Jayesh, I'm Lisa from Dreams Launched Agency. We've introduced a platinum package that you'd be interested to know about. You get a free portfolio plus behind-the-scenes video footage, full representation, personalized mentorship programmes and even endorsement deals on TikTok. All this for only Rs 11,000 a year.'

She must have worked as a telemarketer before turning into a talent agent. 'Lisa, I've said this before. I'm not interested, and I know that one doesn't have to pay money to get work in the industry.'

'Who told you that? There are no free lunches in life, dear.'

'First, I'm not your dear. Second, enough people have told me this after I mistakenly paid you the first time around. Third, talent agents earn through commissions and not these shady schemes. That's why I think you're a fraud. Call me again and I'll call the cops on you.'

He disconnects and blocks her number. *Such parasites need to be booked for harassment!* But the call gives him an idea—he could play a dancing cop!

Jayesh is looking up references online when his broker calls. 'Ashok, I'll call you back.'

'Sir, one party is interested in renting the Four Bungalows flat with the two-bedroom-kitchen,' Ashok says.

'Renting the entire flat or one of the bedrooms?'

'Only one bedroom, sir. The other one is occupied by that tenant.'

'Why do you call me for such small things? You know what to do—get the paperwork sorted, take a security deposit, etc.'

'Yes, sir.'

'Tell me about this party.'

'She's single, works for an NGO and her name is Miss Meera.'

'Ask her to furnish a joining letter and salary slip as proof. I don't want struggling actors as tenants because they're dodgy about paying rent on time. We've suffered those people enough in the past.' Jayesh hangs up because it's his turn to audition.

* * *

Jayesh sees himself pump iron in the mirror at the gym. '7, 8, 9,' he counts under his breath. His shoulders are like cannonballs, veins bulge from his arms, and his jawline looks even more sculpted because it's clenched. He could pass off as Rocky Balboa!

He lives for the gaze—his own and that of the commoners in the street. TikTok gives him the eyeballs, but nothing compares to an article in the city supplement. The day he comes into the public eye, which is to say, the day he signs his first feature film, he'll invite the press to interview him at the gym. The camera loves a toned body and a photogenic face, while the public swoons over a fit actor. All he needs is one break and a good public relations (PR) team to take care of the rest. '15, 16, 17.'

This is his second workout of the day after his three-hour session in the morning. His form was better then; now, he's a little out of juice. To add to it, today has been a slow day of auditions at Aram Nagar, and none of his trainees have shown up either.

His work as a personal trainer gives him a sense of purpose and extra income. He's learned never to deny any form of Lakshmi. *Money begets money*, as Pappa would say. It was by chance that a college kid who was working out requested him to share some tips, impressed by his form and physique. The kid became his first trainee and the word spread.

That's how Jayesh met Zainab. She'd introduced herself as an actress from Los Angeles, who was here for the love of Bollywood and 'Sharook Khan'. Her accent captivated him. He often smiled when she spoke Hindi. 'Did I say anything funny?' she would ask, making him shake his head.

He still teases her before correcting her pronunciation, but a lot less than he did a year ago. Now his response just makes her see red, as if she has lost her sense of humour.

The door opens and Bidyut walks in with a bounce in his step. His casting agency came into the spotlight when his indie film won the jury prize at Cannes. It was only a matter of time before top-notch production houses hired his services, so he was an important friend to have. The guy recently cast himself in an ad film with Tiger Shroff.

'I tried calling to remind you about Vinny's New Year party tonight,' Bidyut says.

'33, 34. I think I'll pass. I'm pretty spent today.' Jayesh rests the weights on the rack and they fist-bump each other.

'Come for a bit; we can leave quickly. I'm going to Mahabaleshwar tomorrow for my shoot, so I'll be scooting off early.' Bidyut rolls his shoulders. 'I don't see your students, especially your favourite one,' he says with a wink.

'Zainab is at a shoot.'

'For what?'

'It's a dance number for Karmesh production's next feature film.'

'Of course! Mickey Taneja was casting for that. She must be kicked!'

Jayesh nods, adding weights before resuming his workout. '35, 36.'

Until they ran into each other outside an audition room, he had only been a trainer to Zainab. She looked distressed. When he asked her what had happened, she said, 'I've been here a few months and I know what the rents are, but just because I'm a foreigner, they charge me higher rents. Plus, Mumbai houses are such a let-down—cramped spaces and skinny washrooms. I finally found an apartment I like and now the broker's quoting a sky-high price!'

She squinted in the light of the late afternoon sun, so he stepped sideways to shade her. They stood close, facing each other, and he felt a sudden rush of adrenaline. He had seen her training like a beast in the gym but at that moment, she looked so small and helpless that it made him want to protect her.

'These brokers are crooks! Would you like me to speak to him? I know the language of this trade,' he said, squaring his shoulders and running his fingers through his hair.

'That would be wonderful! Thank you so much,' she said with a smile so charming, he heaved a sigh before quickly regaining his composure.

For the first time, Jayesh felt grateful for his experience in the family real-estate business. Those painful years of assisting his father were finally coming in handy. And he wanted to help, to do something to see her perfect ten smile.

He had met Zainab's broker the next day and negotiated a great deal for her. His intervention would help her move out of an aunt's house sooner than she had thought, she told him. She talked about her childhood in Morocco, waitressing and other odd jobs in L.A., and rebelling against her family to become an actress.

He stayed awake all night, thinking of her and how good they would look together.

'44, 45, 46.'

He then hired her broker Ashok to manage some of his Mumbai properties. The man had impressed him with his negotiation skills, and he wanted his current broker to have some competition. He may even be able to find a tenant for his Versova property, which Pappa wanted him to sell though Jayesh preferred holding on

to it—the rent paid for indulgences like his favourite
Diesel jeans which showed off his sculpted glutes.

'56, 57.'

When he wore them to Zainab's house-warming
party, she checked him out for a whole minute, as if
she were undressing him in her head.

When he walked in, he could see many familiar
faces—actors and models he had met during auditions
or at the gym. Bidyut brought him a drink and they
had chatted, though Jayesh kept glancing at Zainab
across the room. Every time he looked at her, she
was looking at him. When the lights went dim and
the music was turned up, it was as if she was dancing
only for his eyes, as she slowly made her way towards
him. Their chemistry was undeniable—a sensation
moved through his body making him feel an ecstasy he
hadn't felt before. In one of Enrique Iglesias' songs,
he remembered, the singer is being lured by a seductress
into a room (most of his songs had a similar theme
anyway). There was a TV channel playing music videos
from the 1990s at the gym—how odd that that should
have come to mind.

The next morning, he woke up in a room with
floral wallpaper and a springy bed. He saw a skirt
hanging from the doorknob, which turned. The door
opened, and Zainab floated out wearing hot pants
and a tank top with her hair dripping. He knew right
then, that with her, it couldn't be a one-night stand.
Days turned into weeks as the heady rush of their
romance shot up. She kept him on the edge—one

moment, she was pulling him into deep waters and the next, she would ghost him for days. Her visits to the gym had become irregular to the extent of dropping out. So the only way to catch her was when she came online.

'59, 60.'

> Would you like to go to the film awards with me? I have an extra pass.

He shot her a text after seeing her online.

He knew her answer would be yes, and that she had been planning to call him as she had insisted on it.

'I've been so busy with dance rehearsals and shoots, I couldn't call you back,' she said when they were at the awards ceremony. 'To make matters worse, my cousin from the States wants to come down to Mumbai for a few months. She's asking me to refer her to producers. What does she think— that I run a talent agency here? Or that they would receive her at the airport to sign her up as a lead then and there? I told her I barely know enough people myself!'

'You have a decent apartment—hosting your cousin shouldn't be a problem,' he said.

'But it's still a one-bedroom house and I want the whole bedroom to myself. My cousin is too spoilt to agree to sleeping on the couch.'

'Then move in with me and let her live at your place. I have two bedrooms; you can take one.' His chest felt tight as he held his breath. He'd made

*her a proposal in spite of himself and was sure
she'd refuse.*

*Her eyes searched his before turning away to look
at the people dancing on stage. A smile crept up her
lips before she said yes.*

He breathes out. '68, 69, 70.'

Zainab is poetry in motion—the way her luscious
hair falls on her breasts during belly dance practice
or her porcelain skin shines from post-workout
sweat. She records herself a lot because watching the
playbacks helps her correct her form and improve.
She posts all her practice sessions on social media. It's
already made her an influencer, which is making some
casting directors take notice of her.

Now, Jayesh too is hooked on making content.
And what a blessing TikTok has been! As an actor,
he can showcase his talent by lip-syncing to famous
dialogues without having to create scenes from his
imagination. Especially after one of his earlier videos
went viral, where he was syncing to Rocky Balboa's
dialogues while lifting weights, the gym has become his
shooting hub too. Zainab often collaborates on videos
with him, though she has been busier since last month.
In the little time that she spends at home, she's either
on the phone or reading aloud to improve her Hindi
diction. He's aware that she is watching him from the
corner of her eye.

'You know I hate that snigger,' she said.

'What? I was yawning.'

'You can't act, so don't even try.'

'That's a bit unfair.' He sat up straight.

'Unfair! Just the other day, you told me that I can't roll my r's so I shouldn't bother trying.'

'No! I said you are good enough as you are. You're beautiful and you dance well—you should focus on that. There'll always be somebody to dub for you if need be.'

'That's the shittiest thing I've heard anyone say.'

'It's a compliment! Why are you fighting with me over silly things?'

'It's not silly, Jayesh. It's triggering to be laughed at like that.'

He got up from the couch as she turned around to walk away and he hugged her from behind.

'I'm sorry. How about I make it up to you? Let's go out dancing to the club at Marriott.'

'I'll pass. I have to meet a friend for coffee later in the evening.'

'76, 77, 78, 79, 80.'

He drops the bar to the floor and lies back, gasping. Sweat streams down his temples into his ears.

Of course, Zainab is equally in love with him. It's another matter that they haven't spoken about it. But it's obvious in the way she continues to stay with him, even months after her cousin returned to the US.

'Hey! I've been calling you,' says Bidyut, throwing a towel at his face. 'You look like crap. Are you okay?' He puts out his hand, offering to pull Jayesh up.

Jayesh crawls on his hands and knees to stand up. He wipes his face and the insides of his ears. 'I'm fine, just pushed myself to the limit today.'

'Go easy, bro. It's the last day of the year. You can't pass out before the celebrations even begin.'

'I barely know Vinny. He's more Zainab's friend than mine, and you're the one telling me about it, not her. It doesn't make sense for me to go,' Jayesh says.

'What's the matter with you? Do you want to ring in 2020 alone? Imagine what'll happen when she comes to the party straight from the shoot and doesn't find you there.'

'How do you know she'll come from her shoot?'

'She . . . messaged me.' Bidyut looks him straight in the eye. 'She must have tried reaching you, but you've barely checked your phone today. Knowing you, that's pretty unusual.'

Jayesh sees a text from her, *but she could always have called him!*

'Have you guys had a fight or something?' Bidyut watches him gulp water from a sipper. 'Bro, get it off your chest. What's the matter?'

'She's been off lately. Even today, we argued before she left in the morning.'

'Why?'

'After Zainab's cousin moved out, I suggested she sublet her apartment, which she did. Today, I suggested she give up the place altogether because there's no point in keeping two apartments. One thing led to another and she started accusing me of bossing her around.'

'Bro, are you for real? You just freaked her out and she isn't even your girlfriend.'

'Of course she is.'

'Are you both exclusive?'

'Isn't it obvious that we are a thing?'

'A thing, yes. But have you told her what you think about her? Has she told you what she thinks?'

'Not really, but she hasn't moved back to her house, which means we are dating.'

'Don't guess, bro, find out.'

'Okay, but what has that got to do with giving up her apartment?'

Bidyut pats him on the back. 'Chill, bro. Get your sorry ass over to Vinny's and we'll talk over a few beers. Also, give the girl a break. She just made it into a Karmesh production. She's probably tripping out.'

As they walk towards the reception, Bidyut says, 'My friend from Mickey Taneja's team told me that Zainab's TikTok numbers worked in her favour. Everybody looks for social media numbers these days. I must say the girl knows how to work her strengths in a country like Bollywood!' They fist-bump and Bidyut opens the door. The wind chimes clang as he walks out.

Jayesh sits on the bench hunched over his knees. He'd been a man about town, with mostly one-night stands and affairs that lasted not more than a week or two, but he had never *lived* with someone and spent as much time as he had with Zainab. *That must mean they are in a serious relationship, right? And so, love would be the most obvious thing, wouldn't it? How stupid of him to not declare his love for her! Maybe he should make a TikTok video as a proposal. No. Is that why she's been so irritable of late? She talks a lot about*

*keeping it casual, but she may actually want it to be
official. Women are so difficult to understand.*

It's too late to simply tell her he loves her; she'll
probably laugh at him. Besides, what if marriage is
the next thing she wants? His career hasn't even taken
off right now; he isn't ready for a commitment as
big as that.

He looks at his phone; it's been two hours since he
checked his TikTok feed.

A couple doing a dialogue re-enactment.

A happy dog greeting its owner at the door.

A kid pulling off a complex skating spin.

. . .

A man dressed in white plastic overalls, looking
like a space cadet, talking about the symptoms of some
flu sweeping through China.

Who cares about that? What's concerning is that
his earlier post isn't getting as many views as he'd have
liked it to. Should he update his feed with a gym selfie?
He looks at his reflection in the mirror. It looks like a
bus ran over him—the dark circles under his eyes are
ugly, and he needs a shave. No amount of Photoshop
filters can fix his appearance. The only thing that will
help right now is a nap. He must get home and rest, or
he won't last the night. He'll make a new post once he's
dressed up for tonight's party.

* * *

A message comes through at the stroke of midnight:

Happy New Year, Mickey! Why aren't you at the party?

'Fuck my life, 2020,' Mickey mutters, putting his phone on silent mode. Notifications continue to pour in, lighting up the screen. He turns the phone face down and sits motionless at his office desk. The room is dark except for the faint flicker of string lights from a faraway hut. He draws the blinds over the French windows.

What are people so merry about? Are they experiencing a New Year for the first time or ringing it in for the last time? Partying on New Year's is for losers. Then that's what he should be doing too. He lost the ASN project; that makes him a fucking loser! They had the nerve to send him an email cancelling the contract, that too, three days before the end of the year.

His head hurts so much that he fears he'll burst a vein. He pulls out his pills while swearing aloud. It took just one false #MeToo allegation against him to make the Americans cancel the contract. *He's no Harvey Weinstein—how dare they insinuate that!* He downs the pill with the dregs of his whisky. He should have seen it coming when Jerry and Carol postponed the meeting twice before finally making it to his office in Aram Nagar.

'*This area has history—it served as a barracks during World War II, thereafter as a transit camp during India's Partition in 1947, and now it houses studios and production offices,*' Mickey told them *as they took in the view of Aram Nagar from his conference room.*

'*Who would have thought?*' *Jerry said.*

'*In a way, I still see this place as the barracks. If you consider the daily battles that hundreds of aspiring actors fight every day just to get an audition or a small role, you too would think that the spirit of the barracks carries on to this day,*' *Mickey said as Jerry's grey eyes scanned the vast, dusty field.*

Jerry had joined ASN seventeen years ago and quickly became a favourite. The shows he had produced had made the network's ratings skyrocket, which is how he'd come to be called the versatile rainmaker. Of the many hit shows he'd produced, *The Dirty World of Derby* was his top-rated documentary of all time. Winning an Academy Award for it cemented his place in the hall of fame. Three years later, his web series, *Have I Seen You Somewhere?* profiled priests, shamans, funeral directors and ghostbusters working day jobs as bartenders, stunt doubles, thrift shop retailers and even porn stars. It had swept most of the Golden Globe awards.

'*That's an interesting observation. Perhaps something we can consider incorporating into B-strugglers.*' *Jerry smiled as Carol nodded.* '*Besides, one can never tell when people's realities become more interesting than fiction. Using that for television makes for delicious programming.*'

'*Speaking of which, my team is working on casting actors as per the brief ASN has shared with us,*' *Mickey said.*

*Jerry pursed his lips before looking him in the eye.
'As you would know, Mickey, we are still finalizing
our people in India. It's a lengthy process because we
don't know the market well enough. Anamika and a
few others familiar with the Indian film industry are
of great help, but let's be absolutely clear. B-Strugglers
is an ambitious project, and our team in New York
wouldn't want the project to be jinxed because of
public perception, especially after Harvey Weinstein.'*

*Mickey crossed his arms and leaned back in his
chair. If only Anamika's family emergency had not
made her reschedule her travel plans, she would've
made these stupid people see the downside of breaking
this deal.*

*'You have to trust in the people you collaborate
with, Jerry. It's a false allegation,' he said, leaning
forward.*

'We believe you, but—'

*'Plus, we've been working on this project for a
while now.'*

*'Unfortunately, we don't take the final calls,' Carol
said. 'The network, sponsors, streaming partners, etc.
are all part of the project and it's a collective decision.
You know how the game works.'*

At 3 a.m., Mickey lights another cigarette. He
blows rings of smoke while watching them rise and
disappear. Showbiz is a smokescreen, and if it requires
him to change how he's perceived by the public, then
of course, he knows how the game works. And he'll
show them how it's won.

Take #8

Bowled Over

'Everyone at the office New Year's party was asking about you, baby,' says Raghu.

'What did you say?'

'I stated the facts! That we've barely spoken since you've been busy auditioning and shifting to your new apartment.'

'Convenient for you to skip mentioning that all we did was argue the few times we spoke, and only because you want me to return to Chennai and fit into the mould of a nine-to-five job and piecemeal acting roles.'

'Look, all I'm saying is—how different could acting jobs in Chennai be from those in Mumbai?'

'Maybe not very different but look at the sheer volume of work and opportunities here! Every audition is like a rehearsal. *The Zombie* was finally picked up by a big production house and now it's doing rounds of festivals, and visibility from that landed me with—'

'Short films are made everywhere; besides they look for *character* actors and you'll find plenty of those roles for yourself in Chennai. It's the mainstream films that are biased towards the conventionally good-looking . . . Your words, not mine.'

Meera paces back and forth in the living room. She misses him when they don't speak, and when they do, the smallest things trigger her. 'Why do you care where I am, anyway? You didn't even bother calling to wish me for New Year's.'

'Relax, I was going to call but you beat me to it. You anger easily now. You know I've missed you terribly, and the only reason I didn't reach out earlier was because I wanted to give you space. I knew you'd call whenever you were ready to talk.'

Raghu is right. She has been irritable with him lately. Surprisingly though, Meera's state of mind hasn't been one of irritability at all! She's been only too happy to have her days packed with auditions, shoots and even discovering her own little routine in preparing for a role—tips that she has picked up from her co-actors and friends in theatre. While this influx of changes should have sent her into a tailspin, it's oddly comforting to roll with the punches that life in Mumbai throws at a newbie. And all along she thought that her comfort zone was being at home in Chennai and specifically in Raghu's presence.

'How are you settling in? And how's your flatmate?'

'Unpacking one suitcase and one carton is hardly any work; the apartment is fully furnished, and Aditi is just lovely! We get along like a house on fire,' Meera says.

'I'm not sure about using that expression any more.'

'You're right!' She laughs. 'Aditi spent a few months auditioning for roles before switching careers, so we have some common ground. Now she works as a community manager at a co-working company. It will make her application for a master's in management (MIM) from New York University (NYU) stronger when she applies next year.'

'Her career switch is the opposite of yours,' says Raghu, treading carefully.

'What's your point?'

'She chose a job that guarantees a salary.'

'We've been through this before, Raghu—'

'I'm not asking you to give up acting altogether, but I still think you had everything going for you in Chennai, with the job and the agency. You just needed to find a better agency.'

'I know that our staying apart has been hard—'

'It takes years of struggle to make it as an actor, Meera, and you're all alone there. What if you're frustrated by the end of it? At least here, we'll have each other's support, and you can pursue acting at your leisure. How long will you punish me with this physical distance between us?'

'It's only for the short term.'

'How can you be sure of that?' he sighs.

'Had I not returned to Mumbai, I would've missed out on the audition that has changed my life.'

'You're talking in riddles.'

'Newsflash! I am acting in Yashika Saini's feature film on the Indian cricket team.' The long silence makes her wonder if the call has dropped. 'Hello? Hello?'

'What? I mean, wow! We've been talking for an hour and you tell me this now?'

'We've been squabbling for the most part, so I waited until now to tell you.' She stretches out on the beanbag. Imagining her first day on the shoot fills her with hope, even as her heart sinks imagining Raghu's expressions at the other end of the line. She's almost sure that he is anything but thrilled.

'When was this?'

'Last week. Patti insisted I have my contract vetted by a lawyer friend before signing.'

'Did you not think it important to share this news with me? Why even bother telling me now?'

'Why are you sulking, Raghu? You objected to my shooting for that zombie film when I was in Chennai, so I wasn't sure how you'd react to this. Besides, you did a vanishing act and were barely available to chat after!'

'Yes, but I ought to be in the know.'

She hears people in the background and a buzzer that goes off at intervals. He must have entered the office canteen. He orders a sandwich before replying.

'I'd only be too happy for you.' He sneezes.

'Are you okay?'

'Excuse me, yes. When do you start filming?' His voice sounds strained and distant. Has he pulled away from the phone? She presses her phone closer to her ear. She wants so much more of Raghu—the hours they spend on calls with each other are simply not enough.

She wants to know why he behaves as if he's losing her. After all, she can also accuse him of shutting her out during his most vulnerable moments, when he just goes quiet. She doesn't hear from him and doesn't even get a response to her messages. On those days, it feels like she's in a relationship with a machine that only responds when forced to. At other times, he smothers her with attention. In Chennai, he insisted on spending every waking hour with her—it was always Meera-o'clock on his watch.

'We start our physical training the day after, and filming in a month and a half around late February. Isn't that great?' She hears the tension in her voice, despite herself. It's incredible how his moods affect hers so much as if they are mirroring each other.

He mutters his agreement.

'Raghu! I really would like to spend more time with you. 2020 would look even more promising if you'd come visit me.'

* * *

The ballroom of a five-star hotel has been converted into an area for costume trials. The girls are still learning each other's names when the assistant director (AD) Esha announces, 'An urgent matter has come up for Yashika so she won't be available for the script reading today. But since she's around the corner, she'll drop by for a few minutes. Please gather here now.'

Radhika, one of the actors, whispers to Meera, 'Sometimes I think these ADs get paid to look perpetually worried and cause alarm.'

The door opens and Yashika Saini walks in with a stately gait. She is leaner in person than she looks on-screen.

'It's been twelve years since she won the pageant, but barely any crow's feet show when she smiles. I bet it's the magic of Botox,' Radhika says, nudging Meera with her elbow.

Yashika smiles, and she and the cast exchange hellos.

'*Bowled Over* is an important story to tell, mainly because there's been no mainstream movie made on the lives of women cricketers,' she says, 'and also because it's my first time as producer.'

A few people in the room cheer and clap.

'We are all very excited, but we are also facing a challenge.' She glances at a middle-aged man standing at some distance from her.

'Atul Kapoor, co-producer,' Radhika says into Meera's ear.

'We were supposed to start production last year, but some unexpected delays made us reschedule. The distributors have offered us a Christmas 2020 release, which still holds. It will be ambitious to wrap up our shoot schedules by mid-June and meet other timelines, but it isn't impossible.' She introduces a man in a tracksuit. 'Roshan is our head coach and he'll brief you on the training format.'

'He's been training Yashika for six months for this role. It'll be even more intensive for us.' This time, Radhika turns around and tells three other girls from the cast as well.

* * *

'So, your day in the sun has finally begun, chellam!' Patti says after Meera recounts her early-morning cricket practice and gym workouts.

'Aiyo, Patti, this is such ninja-level training! In a month, I've developed both muscle and a deep tan.'

'But that's great, no?'

'Yes, but on some days, all I want to do is lie in a tub of hot water.'

'Are you applying that herbal oil? It's very effective on sore muscles. I'll send you more. You can give some to Yashika Saini also, with my regards.'

'Patti, why are you coughing? Are you all right?'

'I strained my voice singing last night. Shashi *Attai*[12] had thrown a karaoke party at her place and I couldn't resist belting out a few of my favourites. I'm gargling and will be fine in no time.'

'Sounds like you girls had a fun night! My table read with my co-actors was fun too. Yashika is friendly, though she's mostly preoccupied with paperwork and creative decisions.'

'That would be so, wouldn't it? Being a first-time producer must be extra work.'

'Yes, but even after all these years, it seems like she is desperate to prove herself with this film.'

'Wanting to prove ourselves has nothing to do with the passage of time; it's human nature.' Patti's voice sounds croaky.

'Is that why you sang so much last night?'

---

[12] Aunty.

'Shashi challenged me to a duel, that too in the presence of Mr and Mrs Krishnan, their children, and their grandchildren!'

'I'm surprised you never acted in films, Patti.'

'I know you mean it as a wisecrack, but let me tell you—in our times, the industry was entirely male-dominated. Sometimes, the only woman on a shoot would be the actress. I read in an old magazine article that actresses did not even have separate bathrooms.'

'I can't imagine that. In my case, we are so many women that I wish my character had a love interest.'

Through the glass door, Meera can see Yashika pacing and talking on the phone. The cast is already speculating that the film's release will be pushed to the spring of 2021.

Aditi's name flashes on the caller ID.

'When are you coming home?' Aditi whispers.

'What happened? Has someone died? Why do you sound so serious?'

'Raghu is here, in the living room. Looks like he wants to surprise you.'

'What? I'll be another hour . . . You guys can chat meanwhile. I'll make a quick stop at the grocers. Anything you want?'

'Get some booze from the liquor shop next door and I'll order in some dinner.'

Meera hangs up, smiling to herself. Raghu is outdoing himself with the surprises—he sure loves to throw a ball at the stumps every now and then. She shakes her head at the thought—that's enough cricket jargon for the day!

Going home, she hums the film's theme music in the auto. It had played on a loop at the studio and now is playing in her head.

'Have I seen you in a TV commercial recently?' the shopkeeper says, placing her items in a bag and handing her the change.

Meera nods. She is already being recognized, and she hasn't even begun shooting her film yet!

'SWIM dishwashing soap.'

'Aha!' The shopkeeper snaps his fingers imitating her gesture in the ad. She imagines him mimicking her swinging a bat after *Bowled Over* releases in theatres.

Raghu opens the door saying, 'There you are!'

Meera throws herself into his arms. Everything about him feels so familiar, just like home—the smell of his perfume, the grip of his embrace, the questions in his eyes. She looks up at him. 'Just like I'd imagined—you welcoming me at the door when I return from work.'

He gives her a half-smile. 'What took you so long?'

'I had errands to run, but what made you surprise me?'

'There's no official holiday for Valentine's Day, so I took the day off to come and see you.'

'You meet me after four months, and only for an extended weekend?'

'I know, baby, but I'm the one with the real job here.' He laughs loudly to fill the sudden silence in the room. 'The real *boring* job, I mean . . . Will you still show me off as your main squeeze at your movie's premiere?' He kisses her neck and slides his hand under her shirt.

* * *

'We finally begin filming today. Fingers crossed that *Bowled Over* will be 2020's biggest hit!' Yashika breaks open a coconut by slamming it on the concrete floor. The team erupts into claps, whistles and chants of '*Ganpati Bappa Morya*!'[13]

As Yashika looks for a spot boy to hand the fruit to, Dabloo reaches her. If he's among the first to grab the broken coconut, he is sure to be blessed. Ideally, he would like Bappa to give him an acting offer, but in dire need of cash, any odd job will do just fine. He breaks the coconut into pieces, offering the tray of prasad to the cast and crew.

The director, Yashika and each cast member mumble a prayer as they pick up a piece. He recognizes some of the cast—this one was the lead actor's sister's friend in *Aasmaan* and this one is the 'Aha' girl from the SWIM dishwashing commercial.

'Dabloo! Where is director sir's fruit bowl? You moron, you leave your chores midway and I'm the one who gets shouted at,' says Mangat, another spot boy.

'Arré, his assistant took the fruit bowl to give to the director. How am I to blame if the assistant didn't do so? Don't teach me my job. Now get lost.' Dabloo swings the empty plate on his way back to the snack counter. This Mangat fellow is the pits, always putting him down in front of others.

---

[13] An endearing term used to refer to Lord Ganesha, the deity for good luck and remover of obstacles. It is similar to saying 'Hail Lord Ganesha' or 'Praise Lord Ganesha'.

'Spot!'

Dabloo turns around.

'Your name's Dabloo, right? Can I get a cup of coffee, please? I'll be in the green room,' says the SWIM dishwashing girl.

It's polite of her to ask his name, otherwise actors these days don't care to look beyond their own staff. They can barely remember their dialogues, let alone crew members' names.

He must find out her name. If there's one thing he has learnt serving actors on sets, it is to address them by their name—actors love the sound of their name—and also to serve them fast. If he knows they'll have to wait for their order, he lets them know immediately.

'Meera ma'am, coffee.' Dabloo walks in holding a short steel glass. She's leaning on the couch while two actors on folding chairs get their hair and make-up done.

'Filter coffee! I didn't know we had that on set. More importantly, how did you guess?'

'Some crew members like this, so production stocked it. I thought you might like to try it. But I can bring you something else in no time.'

He sees her eyes close as she takes a sip. Is that a smile? Maybe she's reminded of some place or someone. He has seen tea and coffee do this to people, as if these aren't common drinks but an emotion.

'This is perfect, Dabloo. Make it for me every day.'

'I make excellent chai also if you want it. I can make it according to your preference. I can even make extra sweet, spiced cutting chai. It's my favourite,' he says, fidgeting with the tray. Telling her his preference feels like an intimate revelation.

Esha comes in and says, 'We want Radhika, Bhavna, Meera and Nupur now. This is a long shot so don't waste time with touch-ups and just make a dash for the set. Spot, bring me nimbu paani.'[14] She leaves, arguing with someone on her walkie-talkie.

'These ADs could teach us a thing about running between the wickets,' Radhika says, making the others laugh as they walk out towards the stadium.

The stadium comes into full view as Meera walks out. She scans the breadth of it. It's a clear day and the late February sun feels warm even though there's a nip in the air. A drone is hovering a few metres above her while the operator testing it stands near the monitor. Next to him is Tanuj Bhat, the film's director, giving actors instructions over a loudspeaker.

His last movie as director was also female-driven, and it pleased both the critics and the audience, especially women. It also led to an online magazine article dubbing him 'The Ladies' Man'. Hopefully, he'll work the same magic with this film too.

Meera jogs to her position near the boundary; the grass feels like a thick carpet. She stretches as she waits for instructions. For a moment, it's as if she's back

---

[14] Lemonade.

at Mickey Taneja's office, looking out the window. Everything is moving so quickly. *Is this too good to be true?*

* * *

Yashika's hair is being braided as she talks to her co-producer, who's reflected in the mirror she's facing. 'There's a lot at stake, Atul ji. We cannot halt shooting for a few days because of some flu. We're already running late.'

'But we'll have to take precautions. This is supposed to be a deadly flu. My wife is already panicking. She says that the situation in China is eerily similar to the situation in the movie *Contagion*, and it's spreading like nobody's business,' says Atul, scrolling through his phone. He had previously backed mostly masala movies and slapstick comedies, but given that sports films and biopics have become a marketable genre, he was quick to co-produce this project.

'Atul ji, it's the media's job to create panic whether or not there is any reason for it.'

'That's what I told my wife; we Indians have such good immunity, nothing can affect us. But she insists she has a bad feeling. Tell me, what can I do about women's instincts? She's always imagining the worst. The other day she was crying over the phone, begging our son to return from London . . .'

'I must prepare for my scene now. Can we talk at lunch?'

'Sure but we'll have to arrange for sanitizers and face masks for the crew. It's best to take precautions.'

'A waste of money, in my opinion, but I'll leave the decision to you.' Yashika takes a selfie of her braided hair while asking her assistant to open the script to her scene and hand it to her.

Take #9

Dropping the Ball

'Just as I was leaving the grocery store, someone walked in from the back door with a tray of freshly made gujiyas.[15] I couldn't resist packing a few for us.' Aditi is lounging on the couch. 'This is the closest I'll get to celebrating Holi this year.'

'But these are a bit too syrupy; I'm sure your aunt in Pune makes them better.' Meera takes a bite of the gujiya and puts it back on the plate.

'Oh, the best! I asked Nita *maushi*[16] to send a box, but she was slightly ill because of the changing season. And my cousin who was to visit me dropped his travel plans at the last minute. Who would have thought the

---

[15] A sweet, deep-fried pastry and a popular dessert during the festival of Holi.

[16] Mother's sister; aunt.

festival would be so subdued this year? It's so dull that everyone's holed up in their homes.'

'People are afraid the virus could transfer from water balloons and colours because they're made in China!' Meera says, sinking back into her beanbag.

'I never got around to asking you this, but how did you arrange for the joining letter and salary slip to show to our *stud-boy* landlord, Jayesh?'

'A friend of Raghu's works at an NGO here. He helped.'

Aditi giggles and says, 'Imagine Jayesh's face when he sees you on the big screen. He'll join an NGO too if he thinks casting agencies audition from there.'

'The nerve of the guy—disqualifying actors as tenants when he's an aspiring actor himself!'

'This reminds me, Raghu told me he was upset about your decision to move to Mumbai.'

'What else did he say?' Meera leans in.

'That the long distance has made you somewhat distant towards him.'

'Wow, that's a lot to say to a stranger! We've had enough arguments about my career change, but to tell you that?' Meera is taken aback. 'Raghu confounds me—there are days when he's so understanding, and then in a snap he'll say something highly insensitive.'

'Maybe he's looking for a reaction from you or trying to make you feel guilty.' She looks Meera in the eye. 'It was my ex-boyfriend's favourite ploy.'

Meera sinks further into the beanbag. This was passive-aggressive behaviour. But Raghu can't be that person. From the time they first met, he had insisted they were soulmates. He hadn't shied away from declaring her as the one he would marry, and nothing had made her feel as cared for as that declaration of his. It promised to fill the void in her heart created by Amma and Appa's physical and emotional absence from her life.

Raghu and she have had undeniable chemistry, and their conversations, for the most part, have been great too. But of late, he's become more unreasonable than usual.

'I'm hosting a few friends for dinner on 24th March,' says Aditi, pulling Meera out of her trance.

'Of course, it's your birthday!'

'It's Tuesday, so it won't be anything wild, and we'll wrap up early. Okay with you?'

'So long as there's cake!'

* * *

Yashika flings the newspaper on her dresser. 'Looks like the film will be *bowled out* of theatres even before its release. Goddamn this coronavirus!'

'Don't lose heart. We'll find a way . . .' says Atul.

'Lose heart? I'm freaking out! It's already 21st March, and if we stop shooting now, what about the loan we've taken? You know how hard it is to get backers for female-centric films.'

'Let's continue shooting but quietly,' Tanuj suggests, sipping his tea. 'We'll shoot with limited cast and crew, follow safety protocols, fumigate the grounds, sanitize the indoor set, and hire extra cabs to pick up and drop everyone.'

'It'll be an added expense—' says Yashika.

Tanuj cuts her off. 'But it's in the interest of completing the film. I'll rework the shooting schedule with the team and make new call sheets.'

* * *

As he brings the coffee, Dabloo notices Meera eyeing the plate of fruit that Nupur, her co-actor, is devouring. Nupur has been complaining that she bloats so much during her period that she has to follow a fruit diet to offset it.

'Meera ma'am, would you like some fruit also?'

'No, I . . . never mind. Just leave the coffee here and bring me a toothpick.'

She takes a toothpick from the box he offers her and walks up to Nupur. As they chat, she has some pieces of papaya.

She believes the superstition that eating from a menstruating woman's plate would please the period gods, compelling them to make an appearance. Given that she's been perpetually troubled by erratic periods, Meera has stopped drawing the line between science and superstition and is willing to try any solution.

Even as she complains about her body aches to Nupur, she reminds herself to tell Patti to stop sending the herbal pills. They were meant to regulate her cycles but haven't worked.

'The aches are possibly due to the strain from long hours of filming. Speak to the coach or physician if it persists,' says Nupur.

'I think it's the early-morning call times. Now that they've rescheduled some of my scenes, I must sleep well tonight or I'll look sucker-punched in my close-ups tomorrow.'

Meera reaches for her phone to see who's calling and is surprised to see that it's Aditi, who doesn't usually call during office hours. When she hears what Aditi has to tell her, her gasp stills the chatter in the room.

'My flatmate's aunt passed away due to Covid-19, and she's about to catch the bus to Pune,' Meera announces amid the silence.

Reactions erupt from everyone. Some gasp, others voice their thoughts.

'She mustn't go.'

'What if she gets infected?'

'No way! Because of the virus, really?'

'Aditi insists on attending her cremation. She was her favourite aunt—Nita maushi. I can't believe the lady is dead!' Meera drops into a chair. *Could her body aches be a symptom of the virus?* She should see the physician on set. But she doesn't have a fever or any of the other symptoms. She decides to wait till after her scenes have been shot—an ill-timed move could jeopardize her career.

* * *

When the doorbell rings, Meera sits up with a jolt. She fumbles for the light switch, wondering who could be ringing her doorbell at 3.20 a.m. It rings again, for longer.

She looks through the peephole, opens the door and says, 'What the hell, Raghu? You gave me a fright!' She drops the knife she was holding.

'Surprise! I tried to get an earlier flight, but this Covid thing has disrupted all schedules. Sorry to frighten you, but I wanted to see you, never mind the risk to me.'

Meera is adjusting her eyes to the light, trying to make sense of Raghu's explanation. 'What's in your hand?'

'I couldn't find flowers to say, "I'm sorry", so I got a cauliflower instead.' He smiles. 'There was a convenience store open on my way here.'

'Is this what you're going to do each time we have a fight?' She turns to walk back to her room.

'You've become so aloof, Meera. It's hard to talk to you on the phone so I thought of coming this weekend to resolve our issues for good.'

'Couldn't you at least have informed me?'

'You like surprises, don't you?'

'Not the ones I get at ungodly hours. It's a big day on the set today, and if I don't sleep well, I'll look like a beast on camera. You know that!'

'Calm down, baby. I'm sorry. I tried catching an earlier flight but the tickets were too expensive.'

'Didn't you say something about the flights being rescheduled?'

'That too,' he says, flinching at being caught out. As he moves close to her, she stops him.

'I just meant to give you a goodnight hug. You should get some sleep,' he mumbles.

She lies still in bed, her back to Raghu. His visit has startled her; sleep is impossible even though the corners of her eyes feel heavy. She'll continue to pretend to be asleep lest he want to get intimate.

* * *

Meera's phone beeps—it is the reminder she'd set for Aditi's birthday, 24th March. Poor girl—she must be miserable because of her aunt!

Meera looks into the mirror at her ungainly eye bags, the result of all the crying and fighting of the past three days. If only she had slammed the door in Raghu's face when he'd showed up in the wee hours of the morning, at least she wouldn't have had to deal with his tantrums over the weekend! When she had declined a dinner date on Saturday, he accused her of behaving like a star. She had told him on dozens of occasions in the past that she needed rest and time to herself in the middle of an important project in order to deliver a good performance, and that she wasn't being a diva. But he just didn't understand that everything in her life did not revolve around him. It was pointless to repeat everything all over again—the man continued to overstep her boundaries without so much as even acknowledging her genuine concerns. Like, he just didn't get that she did not appreciate his late-night surprise. Eventually, she felt so provoked that she said the unthinkable.

'I want to break up with you.'

It must be her exhaustion from the shooting and her impending period (the false-alarm trips to the toilet had contributed as well). But who's to help him understand this?

Teary-eyed, he had begged her to reconsider. She had never seen him this emotional, but she was strangely unmoved. She even felt no remorse about lying to him about having her period, just to avoid his sexual advances. For once, her hormones were working for her, making her less emotional and more logical.

'Looks like you were so excited rehearsing your part that you forgot to sleep!' says Radhika.

When Meera tells her about Raghu's surprise visit, she says, 'How romantic! He must be crazy about you to travel at a time like this.'

Meera's smile does not reach her eyes. She has downed her third cup of coffee yet her head feels fuzzy when she's called to shoot. Bat in one hand, helmet in another, she drags herself to the stadium. Her feet seem to have swollen inside her shoes, making them tight and uncomfortable to walk in. It's become much hotter suddenly, and there's a stillness in the air. Such a contrast from the usually pleasant, windy days of March. Sweat dampens the back of her neck—it's hard to wipe it off under the collar with her gloves on. She rubs her shirt like she wants to rip it off. Her chest is heaving from the exertion of walking to the crease. She looks around—there are massive green screens lining the field's periphery that will be used to superimpose a crowd in the edit. Should she explain her condition to someone or can she manage with resting between shots? She signals for water as the crew makes final adjustments to the cameras and lighting.

Tanuj's voice calling 'Action' echoes in her ears from far away. The ground sways beneath her, blurring her vision. Why is the bowler hurling two leather balls at her instead of one? She raises her bat to hit them but loses control and drops to the ground, vomiting before curling into a foetal position.

She sees people running across the field towards her before her vision goes completely blank.

Take #10

Be Positive

The tension is palpable as Yashika paces the length of the van. She should have resisted the urge to rush the shoot. 'If something happens to her, I'll have blood on my hands,' she says, dabbing her nose nervously with a tissue.

'Calm down, Yashika. You're imagining the worst. Be positive! Most likely, the doctors will confirm it's nothing more than exhaustion,' says Atul, more to reassure himself than with conviction. He looks at Tanuj, whose suggestion it was as director to complete shooting on schedule by filming secretly.

'No one from the cast or crew should be allowed to leave till they've been tested for Covid. I've called a lab; they're sending someone over soon.' Tanuj confirms on his walkie-talkie that security has understood his instructions before he looks at Atul. 'We should have arranged for an ambulance on standby.'

Atul throws his hands up in the air. 'There's a shortage of ambulances. At least I got a vanity van to act as a makeshift ambulance. Besides, everything costs twice the market rate!'

'Please Atul ji, let's not worry about expenses at this point. We must do everything we can to prevent this news from reaching the media.' Yashika shudders at the thought of even one article about the incident.

'I'll do what I can but keep your publicity team on standby for a possible clarification. The question is, what do we say? We shouldn't have filmed secretly in the first place.'

'We have an update,' says Tanuj as he climbs into the van.

Yashika hadn't noticed him step out. She clasps her hands together. 'Was it someone from the press?'

'No, it was the physicians attending to Meera. Her pulse and temperature are normal, and her oxygen is at ninety-seven. The good news is that she has tested negative for Covid.'

Atul exhales with relief and Yashika collapses into a chair. 'So why did she faint today?'

'They believe it's dehydration or physical exhaustion. She regained consciousness soon after they put her on saline. They've done a rapid antigen test but are awaiting the results of the polymerase chain reaction (PCR) test from the lab. Atul, you'll have to arrange for her to quarantine at a hotel.'

'Says who, Tanuj? She's a local and can isolate at her own house. We need to be as low-key as possible.'

The worry line reappears on Yashika's forehead. 'Should we send her off right away in a cab?'

Atul shakes his head and instead asks for the driver of the vanity van to be brought to him.

* * *

'Meera, you haven't told us how your movie prep is coming along.' Aditi's words were slightly slurred.

'Either you haven't been listening to me over the past few days, or you're so sloshed that you can't remember.'

'Actually, I was asking so that Raghu would know.' Aditi rose from the sofa. 'But you're right, I am smashed. I must go to bed before you start round three of your drinking game. Good night, lovebirds. Happy Valentine's Day again.'

Raghu watched her stagger to her room before speaking in a low tone, 'I think Aditi is jealous of you.'

'She's not. She's quite comfortable in her skin.' Meera's emphatic gesture jerked her hand forward, spilling some wine from her glass.

'I don't mean professionally. She's been watching me so closely that it looks like she's got the hots for me.'

'She's a good listener. Plus, I talk so much about you, she's just curious to know you better.'

Raghu took another swig. 'What's our next drinking game?'

'It's an improv game we've played during rehearsals—without the drinking, of course. It's called

"Questions Only."' She poured the remaining wine into her glass.

'One person asks a question and the other person answers with another question, and so on. If you answer with a statement, then you take a sip of your drink. Ready?'

'Have we begun?'

'Good.' She took a gulp. 'Your turn.'

'Let's see.' He scratched his beard. 'Do you have any hidden talents?'

'Do you think playing cricket is a talent?'

'What else can you play?'

'Whatever you want,' she chuckled and swallowed a mouthful slowly.

'Which is your favourite TV show?'

'Would you even call Mera Parivar a show?'

'You're right! It's such a waste of prime-time television. I regret having acted in that show.' She took a sip. 'What's your pet peeve?'

'People asking me to get married,' he said, taking a sip. 'What's your guilty pleasure?'

'Thinking about our wedding.' She winked at him, knocking back the rest of her drink.

'Clearly, we aren't going anywhere with this game, Meera. Might as well move to the bedroom.'

'We should do something wild, Raghu! What do you say we just get married right now?' She laughed.

'You're as smashed as your friend, baby,' saying this, he picked her up. 'Let's make babies tonight. We can marry some other day.'

'Ha! Look who's pretending to be drunk now! But I know you barely drank anything.' She hummed as he carried her to the bedroom.

* * *

Meera squeezes her eyes shut. The only way to ease her fears is to take the test. Through the window of the vanity van, she sees a chemist's shop coming up. 'Stop here for a minute, please,' she calls to the driver as she ties a scarf around her face.

The chemist sees the vanity van stop. A woman wearing a veil and sunglasses walks in.

'Is that a filmi van?' he asks her.

'What does it look like? I want a pregnancy test kit.'

She could be a famous actress trying to hide behind that scarf, he thinks, but what a show she's making by driving about in that make-up van. These film industry people not only have loose morals, but they are also desperate for attention even in a crisis!

If only he could get a peek inside the van, he might find a clue to her identity. Some film stars surround themselves with their own photos. He ambles outside the shop as she leaves but barely manages a glimpse before she slams the door shut. Disappointed, he goes back to his place behind the counter.

At the door to her flat, Meera's hands are shaking so badly that she can't even turn the key properly. Her heart is pounding, and she takes a deep breath to steady herself. Once inside, she rushes to the bathroom.

Positioning the dropper over the sample well, she prays for one line to appear. There's no way the test can be positive; she's been on contraceptives due to her PCOS for far too long. It's probably a delayed period, with dehydration playing additional havoc.

As she looks, two dark lines appear, at which point, all lines, shapes and forms blur together.

II

Action!

Act one

Take #11

Lock, Stock and Barrel

Sunil is jostling for space, trying to find his result on the college noticeboard. Each time he gets close, he is pushed back. He decides to check later and is about to leave when he sees Kanika, who had joined last semester but is already the most sought-after girl. He watches her crane her long neck, calling out her roll number for someone else to find it on the noticeboard. He must grab this chance; he pushes through the crowd once more, this time, with all his might.

Jayesh has read the script a few times to absorb the scene, but the casting supervisor keeps calling his performance a caricature.

'Try and remember the last time you were so stunned by something or someone that your jaw dropped to the floor. Focus on that feeling when playing Sunil. Last take.'

What does a smitten lover look like, if not a hero from the movies? Jayesh wonders. There are as many variations to that bewitched expression as there are shades on a wall paint colour catalogue. There's no room for any more experimentation, yet this supervisor is bent on reinventing the wheel.

Just then, a man barges into the room. 'Did you hear the news? A nationwide lockdown is being imposed from midnight. It'll be a total ban on public movement, like a *janta*[17] curfew but more stringent.'

'For how long?'

'Twenty-one days.'

'A lockdown even for film shoots?' Jayesh's eyes widen.

'Everything will be shut—offices, shops, restaurants, some say even public transport. I've heard that grocery supplies are flying off the shelves. I won't get any if I don't leave now,' he says, dashing out of the room as suddenly as he had entered.

The casting supervisor knows that postponing production will delay his fee payment as well.

'What about this audition?' Jayesh is worried. He's been at his A-game at auditions lately. This lockdown has come just when he could win the role he's most suited to play—that of the college hunk.

The casting supervisor whistles softly. 'Your guess is as good as mine. But we'll do the last take. React to

---

[17] Public.

my cue just the way you did on hearing the news about the lockdown. That's the look I want!'

* * *

A woman, her face muddied except for patches which her tears have washed clean, is sitting on dry, cracked land. She is singing with all her heart, a song that seems to be aimed at the cloudless skies. Eventually, she feels water around her toes, then her thighs and, finally, her waist. It lifts the boat she's been leaning against. 'It's a miracle,' she cries, only to realize that the water is the tears she had shed while praying for rain.

Was that woman singing one of Amma's poems, sprinkled with themes of grief and loss? Meera wipes the tears from her cheeks. This vivid dream is one of the few she recalls upon waking. It's dark outside; she has probably woken up earlier than usual. The phone shows 9.55 p.m. She's shocked to see it's the end of the day. The pregnancy test kit is on the floor—it must have fallen after she cried herself to sleep this afternoon. She stiffens again as she tries to recall Valentine's night but her memory is foggy after Raghu carried her to the bedroom. She should have popped a birth control pill the next day instead of aspirin for a headache. Why had Raghu not warned her? He'd had hardly anything to drink that night. How could he put her at such risk? Anger shoots through her body.

She tries calling him but there's no signal. She wonders what the problem could be—she paid her bill just last week. Meera reboots her phone, data settings and mobile network, but there's still nothing—the device is lifeless. The only other time such a service outage had occurred was last year, due to a short circuit at the phone company's base station. What could it be now?

She steps outside, hoping the phone will connect with a free public network somewhere. As she walks around, she notices that the entire neighbourhood seems to have queued up outside the grocery store. Is the owner distributing free stuff at 10.30 p.m.? Why does everyone look panic-stricken? She joins the queue behind an elderly man and asks him what's happening.

'Didn't you watch the news? The prime minister has announced a total lockdown starting at midnight. People can't step out of their houses without a government pass. Even gatherings have been limited to about eight to ten people.'

She gasps.

'Yet, look at the crowd here. Everyone is stocking up. My daughter and son-in-law are on their way to pick me up. They said, 'Papa, you will not stay alone.''

The sound of an ambulance siren in the distance could very well be the alarm bells ringing in her head. Should she wait in line or rush to the hospital? Who's going to consider her request for an abortion at this hour? How is she going to step out for an abortion at all in a lockdown? Her hands go cold at the thought.

'Will—will hospitals be open for general cases?' She asks the old man.

'My friend just went to the hospital, and she said they're flooded with Covid cases. They have no time to see other patients,' says a woman in her late thirties who's standing behind Meera. 'Unless there's an emergency, it's best to wait it out.'

Meera still doesn't have access to a network. She asks the woman, 'Could you lend me your phone's hotspot for a minute, please? It's urgent.'

'My username and password are the same as my name, Lisa,' she says, eyeing Meera intently, who is now wrapping a scarf around her face. 'Were you in that television commercial for SWIM?'

Meera nods absently.

'I run the talent agency called Dreams Launched. You can check us out on Instagram. I might have a project for you. Give me your number and I'll call you in the coming week.'

Meera looks at her in disbelief. Of all her interactions with talent agencies, this one has to be the worst—in a queue at the grocer's at the start of a pandemic, when what she desperately needs at the moment is a gynaecologist. Though she manages to top up her internet plan (again!), her WhatsApp messages aren't going through, and the only calls she can make are to customer care. But even as she's trying to resolve the issue, she's thinking of Patti. She's an old woman; it'll be difficult for her to manage without the maid who also doubles as her errand girl. What if there is an emergency? With the closure of flights and trains, they can't even visit each other.

When the fourth customer care agent asks her to explain the issue all over again, Meera starts shouting at her. Luckily, the scarf covering her mouth muffles her voice, and she regains her composure and airs her complaint.

It's been almost an hour of waiting in the queue. As she looks up from her phone, she sees the elderly man walk out of the store. He turns to her and says, 'They are almost out of supplies. The shopkeeper's staff has gone to bring the remaining stock from his godown. The last time I saw something like this was during the 1971 war!'

Back home, Meera sees that carrying the grocery bags has left deep marks on her fingers. She hears multiple beeps as the notifications flood in. Her connection has finally been restored! She scrolls through the missed calls and messages from Patti, Aditi and . . . Raghu.

His messages read:

> You are unreachable, baby, please call me back. Are you all right? Did you hear the news?

All of a sudden, she feels the anger spread through her body again like fire. She has news to give him too.

* * *

'My chai will be cold by the time you bring me the newspaper. Where is it?' Mickey asks his housekeeper.

'Lockdown, sir. No paper.'

No paper?! Oh no! So, three more weeks of no newspapers in the morning? Mickey takes a gulp of tea, flinching as it burns his tongue. Starting his day without the newspaper is going to take some getting used to. But maybe he shouldn't be fretting about it. It's not like he's been receiving any flattering press of late. If anything, Covid and the lockdown will keep him out of the news for some time so people can forget about the allegation against him, and he'll get the time and space to plan his next move. No more paparazzi chasing him around town or media channels thrusting their mics in his face—the universe has really cut him some slack! He sighs and takes a small sip.

Scrolling on his phone for news, he sees an update about ASN's plans to partner with a digital streaming service to create original content since the 'quarantine lifestyle' has resulted in a major shift in the viewing preferences of audiences around the world.

He fires up one end of a cigarette and exhales slowly. Something tells him this might not be the time for him to lie low. He needs to work on revamping his image. His experience in the film industry had led him to never rule out the possibility of a re-connection in relationships, no matter how definitive or bitter the end might seem—because friendships and enmities are always open to negotiation when obscene amounts of money and ambitions are involved. How different could Hollywood possibly be from Bollywood in that respect?

* * *

Dabloo's heart sinks to his stomach when his roommate tells him that the lockdown is likely to be extended for another month. The roommate's father is a peon in a government office in Delhi, and he made Dabloo and the others promise not to share the news with anyone.

'Not possible; anything made in China hasn't been known to last too long,' someone in the room jokes.

While his roommates scamper in and out of the main door, some heading out to buy enough food and essentials and others walking in with loaded plastic bags, Dabloo tries calling his previous employer, the security company that had hired him as a watchman but refused to pay his pending salary. If they agree to pay him, he can sustain himself for a while. As expected, his call goes unanswered.

It's 2 a.m. before everyone settles on their cots, though they must also be struggling to sleep. He'd barely had two coins to rub together when he found work as a spot boy in *Bowled Over*. The film was being made by a reputable production house, but experience has taught him that the most renowned studios are the worst paymasters. And the first ones to be thrown under the bus when a film is delayed or shelved are those at the bottom of the rung. He's been awake the entire night trying to find a way to resolve the situation. It's a little before 4 a.m., his usual time to wake and so he does, only to realize there is no work to go for.

The house is still, with the only sounds being the three different kinds of snoring in his room and in the hall. He has gotten used to his neighbour's snoring. Its rhythm puts him to sleep on most nights—except tonight. Though his eyelids are heavy, he stays awake wondering how he will pay next month's rent, should the lockdown be extended. As he fiddles with the Hanuman pendant around his neck, a gift from Bindu bhaiya just before he boarded the train to Mumbai eight years ago, he recalls their conversation from the evening before: 'This *Karona* virus is just a hoax. Precaution is fine, but why this lockdown? Remember that story Baba told us about a *shikari*[18] who was walking along a trail and got startled by a shaking bush? He froze because he didn't want to make noise and get killed. And then, guess what came out of the bush? One small squirrel. We humans have become like that shikari—always practising extreme caution. Have you ever heard of anything like this happening before? No, right? Twenty-one days will pass like this,'

---

[18] Hunter.

Dabloo heard him snap his fingers, 'And then life will be back to normal,' Bindu bhaiya had said.

It was unlike Bhaiya to say this. He was always one to err on the side of caution while Dabloo leaped first and looked later. But this time, it seemed as if the roles had been reversed. He's not sure what has brought about this change. He wanted to argue with Bhaiya but the call dropped, and when they spoke again, they began discussing family matters.

As dawn breaks, a new thought emerges—what if the shikari had assumed the shaking bush was a squirrel only to be greeted by a tiger instead? Had Dabloo's own hardscrabble life in Mumbai blunted his edges?

Take #12

Can We Do a Retake?

Jayesh sucks up the last few drops of his protein shake, noisily drawing in the air at the end. It's a great post-workout meal and so easy to make too. Five days of lockdown has made him appreciate small things like these, but at the same time, it has also made him listless.

He tries to keep himself busy by spending most of his time working out, recording himself at different times of the day from different angles or posting and binging on TikTok videos. But thoughts of Zainab always find a way in—when he tries to take a nap, cooks himself a white egg scramble (her staple breakfast) or tries to read the book on acting she left behind.

'Given the speed at which you're driving, I'll definitely reach the airport by tomorrow,' Zainab said to him.

'*I can't go any faster. Seems like everyone is on their way to the airport to catch the last few flights out of India.*'

'*I should've just taken an auto; it would have wound quickly through the traffic,*' she mumbled.

'*It's not as if there's no threat from coronavirus in Los Angeles. I don't see the point in your travelling there to stay safe. You'll see, all the airlines will resume service in a week. This is all hogwash; just a fear tactic to fleece customers like you.*'

'*There's no point in making me feel bad about my decision, Jayesh. Besides, I think we needed a break from each other anyway.*'

'*Are you breaking up with me?*'

'*For the umpteenth time, we were never a couple in the first place. But if that's how you understand it, then yes, it's a break-up.*'

How he wishes he could fly to L.A. and meet Zainab! Even if she slams the door in his face, he could try his luck in Hollywood. She'd once told him that with his wheatish skin and dark hair, he would look like an *exotic creature* among all those Americans, and the agents would pursue him like crazy.

Thoughts of Zainab are becoming his biggest Achilles heel; they distract him to the extent that he forgets the slice of bread in the toaster till smoke is blowing out from the kitchen or he pulls washed laundry out of the machine only to realize he has forgotten to add detergent in the first place. In the moments that he isn't thinking of her, he finds himself daydreaming of being celebrated by the media. 'I eat clean and stay fit, and usually work out for four to five hours a day.' He talks to his reflection in the mirror. It's only a matter of time before he'll be giving interviews to the press. So, it's best to practise his speeches whenever he can. 'Preparing for this role has been my life's biggest challenge; I did not expect the audience to shower me with so much love.' He rehearses a pose while holding the shampoo bottle in the shower.

On stepping out, he hears someone speaking loudly—one of the neighbours seems to be arguing on the balcony—it sounds like the man is complaining to the woman about her cooking while she counters him by calling out his unhelpful behaviour. With everything outside as quiet as death, even somebody clearing their throat sounds loud. It's embarrassing to overhear fragments of their arguments and wonder if any of the other neighbours would ask the two to fight in privacy. He slides the balcony door shut and continues the 'interview'.

The days in the lockdown are dragging, and when not practising pretend interviews and speeches, he keeps himself occupied with selecting outfits that would complement the content he's making. There are so many styles—which one should he put together for his TikTok post? Today cannot be another workout video or a lip-sync. Even the motivational videos can wait. Today, he feels like stepping outdoors, though he'd have to stay within the gates of his housing society.

He sifts through his clothes. *That bomber jacket would be great if he were racing a bike on thin ice, the ice blue windcheater for jumping out of a plane, the khaki green vest for rolling in the grass with lions.* But obviously, he can't record himself doing any of these activities.

He pulls out a plain white T-shirt—something sober to feed the strays. What a noble deed to record! It will win him lots of virtual hearts. Jayesh preens himself in front of the mirror, admiring the slim-fit jeans he's paired with the tee before tearing himself away from his reflection to head out.

'Not even a week into the lockdown and our stray animal friends are wondering where the humans have gone,' he says as he throws biscuits on the street and whistles, skilfully alternating between his front and back camera. 'This is me, Jayesh, signing off. Tag me in your posts when you feed strays. And don't forget to wear your mask, wash your hands and check on your neighbours!' He lifts his own mask for a moment and flashes a victory sign.

He captions it, 'Lockdown diaries, #EpisodeFive'. But before he can upload it, Meera's name flashes on his screen. She must be calling for a rent cut like his other tenants. How many times can he make the excuse that the house is his grandfather's only source of income? If Dado had been alive today, he would have been proud of how his grandson was following his advice of 'money saved is money earned'. He waits for the phone to stop ringing.

* * *

Meera wants to smash her phone against the wall but throws it on the sofa at the last minute. She hasn't been able to speak to anyone at the hospital. When she has gotten through, it has been to listen to a recorded message that is no help at all. Calling gynaecologists listed online has also been mostly futile—they haven't answered the phone. She managed to reach two: one is infected with Covid-19 while the other has given her a tentative appointment two weeks from now. Aditi had referred her to someone, but that person was stuck in a remote location.

She buries her face in her folded arms. Life has been wielding unpredictability like a weapon; each time she feels like she's grown a muscle, some event or circumstance outside her control cuts the entire limb off. God knows what threat an unexpected, ill-timed pregnancy during the pandemic could pose for her if not medically dealt with early enough.

Raghu had not spoken a word when she gave him the news of her pregnancy over a video call. His face had been so devoid of expression that it felt as though she were speaking to a statue. She couldn't tell if he was remembering what happened that night, or if he was trying to come up with an explanation that would excuse his culpability.

Finally, he had said, 'You should have popped a pill the next day.'

'Do you realize how you sound? Those pills aren't candy; they can have serious side effects. They should be taken only if you haven't used protection or in an emergency.'

'Weren't you already on contraceptives for your PCOS?'

'I discontinued them over a year ago. That's not the point!' She had felt her ears go hot and wasn't sure if it was because of the hormonal changes in her body or her anger. How dare he make her solely responsible? Instead of apologizing, he was trying to deflect her questions to justify his irresponsible behaviour. If only she could remember the night more clearly, but she had been sloshed to the gills. There was not much point in talking to him, and she had hung up soon after, saying she had some important calls to make.

Just then, Raghu calls. She digs her fingernails into her palms to prevent herself from refusing the call. She'll leave it unanswered. In fact, it would be best to leave her phone unattended for a while. She can't tell if she's angry at him or at herself.

When the phone rings again, she's praying it's one of the gynaecologists she's contacted, returning her call.

It's Esha, assistant director of *Bowled Over*.

'Meera, how are you feeling now?'

'On top of the world!'

'But your voice sounds raspy.'

'I just woke up from a nap,' she says, wiping a tear.

'You gave us a fright that day! We were so relieved when you tested negative for Covid-19. You must have seen Yashika's messages on the group.'

Meera had fought the urge to ask Yashika for help. Surely a top actress such as her would have access to gynaecologists even during the pandemic. But telling her could result in Meera losing her role. Worse, she would be blacklisted in casting and film circles.

'Shooting will resume in two and a half weeks, the moment lockdown ends. You must follow your workout and diet routines as much as possible, so there's continuity in your physical appearance,' says Esha.

Meera imagines herself in her jersey with her belly protruding. If she doesn't get an abortion soon, the pregnancy will most definitely put an end to her career. Her only option is to visit a hospital and beg for an appointment. The very thought makes fear rise in her throat, making her want to retch.

* * *

Dabloo doesn't know how long he has been lying on his back staring at the ceiling as one of his housemates hums ghazals softly, only pausing to slurp tea from a saucer. There are sounds of cooking and chatting from the kitchen, though no smells yet. Dabloo straightens his arm, numb from being folded under his head. One sideways glance is sufficient to tell him what his other housemates are doing since they share this large single room. Three are asleep, two are huddled over a phone and one is swatting flies as he scratches his crotch. The sounds inside the house are stark against the stillness outside. It's as if the pandemic has given the world a scolding, like the director on a set before the take, and everyone has gone silent.

'What are you staring at? The fan will come down if you try to hang yourself,' says his roommate Utkarsh.

'And then the landlord will trouble you to pay for the fan even after you're dead. I hope the virus gets him before that.'

This sets off a chorus of chatter among the others. Despite their pleas, their landlord hasn't lowered the rent by a single paisa.

'What twisted desire made us move to the city in the first place?' Deepak complains.

Dabloo turns his back to the room and retraces his own journey up to this point.

The sun had shone its brightest the day he had heard about the audition call for a feature film. He had drawn the curtains aside letting the room fill with golden light. Placing his phone on the windowsill, he stood so the light illuminated his face.

A tractor passing by, cyclists ringing their bells and schoolchildren chanting their morning prayer in the distance added to his portrayal of a small-town boy suspicious of his girlfriend's fidelity. It seemed as if the background sounds had been specially orchestrated for his audition. Though the script had needed him to use scornful words, Dabloo had played his character with vulnerability. Perhaps it was the contrasting elements in his performance that had brought him a response from Mickey Taneja's casting agency. He had been so overjoyed at being shortlisted for the role that he decided to go to Mumbai for the final audition instead of sending a recording again.

But how would he convince Ma and Baba to let him go? They wouldn't agree to have his matric education go to waste for a career in acting. He had decided to tell Ma that he'd been hired as a receptionist by a five-star hotel in Mumbai; all she had to do was convince Baba to let him work in the city, instead of assisting him on the farm.

'The employers will pay for my travel and rent,' he'd said, before quietly selling two quintals of onions to afford his train ticket and other expenses.

Bindu bhaiya had been red-faced with anger when he learnt the reason for Dabloo's sleight of hand.

'If you wanted money, you should have asked me. Why did you steal?'

'I didn't steal, bhaiya. It's a loan; I'll return the money once I sign the film.'

'Why didn't you ask me?'

'I was afraid you'd refuse . . . or you would tell Baba about the audition.'

'I can't believe you did all this! And to do what, become an actor? Childhood is over, Dabloo. Grow up!'

'This is the only thing I'm good at; what's wrong with becoming an actor? I don't want to become a farmer like Baba.'

'Who said you must become a farmer? Become my business partner—we'll trade farming equipment and supplies and make good money off it.'

'But a casting office in Mumbai has already shortlisted me for the role of the hero's friend.'

'What if I forbid you to go?'

'Bhaiya, please give me one year. If you don't see me on the big screen by then, I'll do anything you say.'

For his visit to the Mumbai office, Dabloo had worn his best plaid shirt with jeans and a pair of sparkling white shoes that he had purchased at Andheri station. When he had entered Mickey Taneja's studio, a strange smell of talcum powder combined with sweat had hit him. The sheer number of struggling actors waiting in the lobby of the studio made him nervous. He should have sent a recording instead of coming over himself. He had smoothed down his shirt, pushed back his side-swept bangs and vowed to buy himself new clothes from the money he earned from this role.

'I'm here for the audition of Dil Behaal.'

'Name?' the bored young woman at the reception had asked.

'Dabloo, from west Champaran jilla, Bihar.'

She had looked at him like a train ticket examiner would, not saying a word.

'It's the same village as Manoj Bajpayee sir.' There was pride in his voice.

'We don't have your name on our records.'

'Actually, my name is Digambar Prasad Yadav but since everyone at home calls me Dabloo—'

'Weren't you supposed to send us a self-tape?'

'Yes, but I was shortlisted, so I thought it would be better to audition at your studio.' He had dug his hands into his pockets, praying that he wouldn't have to buy a return ticket to his village just yet.

'You should have informed us. I don't know if we— please wait.' She spoke to someone over the phone.

He wondered which of the others had been shortlisted—the tall fellow in the orange shirt or the muscular man with the slicked-back hair. How many were competing for the role—was it a short list or a long list?

Noticing his fidgeting and restlessness, a lady of around his Dadi ma's age, who was sitting near him, said, 'There is nothing to be afraid of, young man. We all make it to the other side of the audition eventually. Just keep at it!'

The spirited Shobhita Chitre had started out just five years ago and had already acted in many TV commercials. 'I audition every day—that is what work for an actor means here. Auditions. If I get finalized for a shoot, great! If not, I go for the next audition. It's as simple as that. Rejection is part of being an actor; you can't take it personally. If you show up consistently, you will have practised your skill enough. Sooner or later, they will be compelled to sign you up. Look at me. I have begun with a head full of white hair.' Shobhita's hazel eyes twinkled as she offered him tea. 'I usually carry this flask and salted biscuits. One can never tell how long one will have to wait for one's turn.'

An hour and a half later, the receptionist had called out his name. 'We aren't conducting the movie audition today, but you can audition for a PSA against smoking. Take the door to the right.'

Days later, the agency had finalized him for the no-smoking advertisement. This came as a relief, *especially after the dismal news that he had lost the movie role. At least he had been signed up for his very first shoot—a PSA that would air on cinema screens across the country. Imagining the pride on Baba, Ma and Bindu bhaiya's faces consoled him a little.*

Lost in his memories, Dabloo pulls his pillow over his ear to drown out the sound of someone humming. Has he made a mistake somewhere in these eight years? Could he do a retake?

* * *

Mickey swirls his whisky as he watches the ice cubes clink.

He was all of twenty-four when he shot Neeraj Mehra's film in the nineties. The tall and ravishing Chhaya Patil had been paired opposite him. After the film's release, a female critic dismissed him with a comment that destroyed his confidence and eventually, his acting career. Her words are still etched in his memory: 'Chhaya, true to her name, has overshadowed Mickey Taneja with both her height and performance. He might just be the worst case of miscasting in the history of Indian cinema.'

It has taken him close to three decades to build himself up as Bollywood's most successful casting director. There isn't a chance in hell that he's going to let yet another woman damage his prospects. He bites into an ice cube as he looks at the skyscraper opposite his. If only he had a pair of binoculars to watch the people within those window frames. It would be like watching auditions of different characters. But these days, the only frames he watches people in are those of a Zoom meeting. There's one with his assistant Reshma and two others scheduled to begin shortly; he had been clear since the beginning of the lockdown that working from home *actually* involved work. Today, they need to decide which marketing and social media professionals they will hire. The ASN project may be lost but he will do everything in his power to reinvent and fortify his brand. Thankfully, since the pandemic has diverted attention from the #MeToo allegation against him, he can plot his next move in peace.

Mickey stubs his cigarette when the phone beeps. It's a message from Anamika:

> The #MeToo accuser is Reshma's friend.
> Watch out!

Take #13

Dolly Shot[19]

Meera reads aloud from the contract, '. . . prohibited from getting pregnant until completion of principal photography of the film . . . a breach . . . which will lead to the dismissal of the actress from the project and/or a claim for damages.' She swallows the lump in her throat. '. . . to mitigate difficulties arising out of . . . expansion of midriff upon pregnancy, not in accordance with the script . . . delays in the shooting schedule . . . leading to financial losses for the producer.'

'Hadn't you read the no-pregnancy clause (NPC) earlier?' Aditi's voice crackles through the phone.

'Of course I'd read it! I just didn't think I would have to read it again.'

---

[19] A tracking shot, wherein the camera moves towards, away from or alongside the subject, which can be an actor, location setting, product, etc.

'Meera, what's done is done! We'll deal with the lawyers or production house later. Did you hear from any of the doctors you called?'

'No, let me call you back. Patti's calling. It could be important.' Meera switches lines to answer Patti's call.

'I just caught you in a rerun of *Mera Parivar* on TV, chellam.'

'Did you seriously put reruns of *The Bold and the Beautiful* on hold to watch that lousy show? Even I wouldn't have done that.'

'My friend called to tell me about it, so I turned on the TV and let it play. At least now your show will not suffer low ratings like it did earlier. Tell me, can you claim royalty from the producers for this replay?'

'No, I was merely replacing an actor for three episodes.'

Long after her conversation with Patti, Meera recalls shooting on the sets of *Mera Parivar*. The interactions from that shoot were so unremarkable; it's irritating that there's a specific nugget of information escaping her memory now.

Meera had been assigned the character of the villain, a visiting sister-in-law who wrecks the harmony between the lead couple. Dressed in brightly coloured saris and dramatic eye make-up, she had spent those eight days mostly sneering at the camera and making her eyebrows dance to the rhythm of her dialogues.

As if that weren't enough, the actress playing the gullible mother-in-law on-screen had made Meera stop in her tracks with her smutty talk. 'You must be hungry after shooting the scene,' she said once, taking a puff from her cigarette. 'Here, eat this banana—it's a gift from Pravin [the cameraman]!' The crew broke into laughter.

At that moment, walking away had seemed like the most sensible thing to do. 'Why, Meera, was it not in good taste?' the actress called cockily as she left.

'That woman is unhinged!' Meera had burst into the green room. 'Is it possible to sue her for harassment?'

Ruchi, the prima donna and lead actress on the show, had put down her make-up brush and looked up at her in slow motion. Since most actors on set had been working on the show since antiquity, they had begun to embody the dramatic expressions and body language of their characters even off-camera. 'What a circus!' Meera had thought to herself.

'No one really considers sexual innuendos by a woman as harassment, darling. Those people are insufferable; just ignore them. You are here for only a few days, then you're a free bird! I'm the one chained to this set. Production makes me work eighteen-hour shifts. I have other things to do—a household to run, visits to make to the salon, to my dermatologist, my gynaecologist. Everything has to be put on hold or delayed indefinitely for this stupid show. I'm sticking around only because they pay well, but the schedules are crazy. Last year, we worked on Diwali and New Year's Eve. Can you believe it?'

Ruchi had suddenly switched to her most honeyed voice while addressing the make-up artist. 'Dada, why don't you use the curling tongs on my hair today? Make it look just like Meera's.'

Shooting for that show was the dullest Meera had ever felt on a set. How could that blip in her career be useful to her condition now? If she's unable to recall that bit of information, then it's probably not important.

She looks at the pages of her *Bowled Over* contract scattered on the table and the sharp lines of her signature on them, especially on the page containing the NPC. These are such watertight clauses; they don't allow for any uncertainty. But who would've imagined the pandemic even a month ago? She paces the room. There must be a way to break out of this cage of misery, and actually fly off like the free bird that Ruchi called her.

Wait a second! Ruchi had also complained about not being able to visit the gynaecologist. That's the nugget she's been looking for!

Ruchi answers the phone after several rings, 'Who's this?'

'Meera. Do you remember me? We shot together for a few episodes of *Mera Parivar*.'

'What do you want?' she says sharply.

'You'd mentioned your gynaecologist. Could you share her number with me? I need some medical advice and I don't know anyone else I can speak to right now.'

'My phone book got deleted. I'll share the contact if I find it,' says Ruchi, before she hangs up.

* * *

Only when his phone battery dies in the middle of watching a prank video does Jayesh look out the balcony door. He hadn't noticed the sky changing colour. He might as well take an evening stroll while his phone charges.

How is it that he has never noticed the bougainvillaea on the porch? It's surprisingly lush. The parking lot is full—a rare sight until the pandemic; all these expensive automobiles including his own, sitting pretty with nowhere to go. Maybe for his next TikTok video, he could wash his car. It does look like it needs a clean-up.

He whistles to the dogs, throwing biscuits on the ground. If Zainab were here, she would have made three meals a day for them. She was crazy enough to talk to her plants. She would have undoubtedly done the same with the strays. He looks at his hand, suddenly wishing she were holding it.

Since when had things started to go south between Zainab and him? Was it the time she cancelled their movie date because of an ad-film shoot?

'How can they give you just a few hours' notice for an all-night shoot?' he had asked, throwing his gym bag to the floor.

'I told them during the audition a few days ago that I would be available today. So, in a way, I have been on notice since,' she had said while brushing her hair.

'But you were rejected for this audition. You and I both know that once rejected, the dates we had blocked earlier automatically get released. What about that?' He had pulled the brush out of her hand.

'Yes, but they called me back and I wanted that part, so I accepted. Such things happen in the industry—you

should know that too! It could be for any number of reasons—the previous actor may have fallen sick, or there may be budget constraints or script changes.' She had begun packing a change of clothes in a duffel bag. 'Why does it bother you so much?'

'Because we had plans for tonight.'

'Look, I'm free to be free and so are you.' She had snatched her hairbrush back and thrown it in the bag.

'A whole year has passed, and a lot has changed since we became flatmates.'

'One thing hasn't.'

'Which one?'

'You are far too possessive for my liking.'

'For your liking? I thought we loved each other.' He had felt his heart sink.

'I like you, but love is too big a commitment for me.'

'Why are you saying this?'

'I don't like being answerable to anyone. And you ask too many questions every day.'

'That wasn't a problem before. Why now?'

'Because I wasn't living with you earlier. I'll say this again: this neediness is the reason I'm afraid of serious relationships; that's why I have to draw the line time and again.'

'Are you sure this is the reason or are you just bored of me? Wait, are you cheating on me?'

'Maybe I should.' She had looked him in the eye.

'What the fuck do you want?!' He had punched the wall.

'Space.'

'*You have your own room for someone in a relationship. How much more space do you want?*'

'*Maybe it's time to get my apartment back from the people I had sublet it to.*' She had slammed the door on her way out.

'Elevators are out of order, sir,' the watchman says when Jayesh presses the button. He would have to climb the eight floors to his apartment; for once, he's glad his house isn't on a higher floor. As he reaches the seventh floor, the door from the lobby to the staircase opens. A woman in her early fifties throws a garbage bag into the chute. It sounds as if the garbage consists of an entire crate of empty bottles. *A drunkard?* he wonders. One of her eyes is discoloured and swollen, and there's an imprint of fingers on her arm. She glances at him before entering house number seventy-two and slams the door shut.

* * *

Dabloo sits on the shore, throwing one stone after another into the ocean, telling himself that the pandemic has not stilled the tide and that this too will pass. He watches the curve of the stones' flight as they hit the water. The splashes remind him of the sound onions made when, as a child, he practised juggling with them, and they fell to the ground.

Baba would often take Bindu bhaiya, his sisters and him to the mela. His jaw would drop watching people cycling on a tightrope, juggling balls and performing acrobatics. His favourite was the clown's act. He was so fascinated by the clown's red nose that he wanted to pinch it and see what it felt like. Once, when Baba had lifted him up to greet the clown, Dabloo had reached for the red spongy ball, pulling it out altogether. Seeing his confusion, the clown had pretended to cry which only made Dabloo cry louder. The clown had pacified him by gifting him the red nose.

It was Dabloo's most prized possession that year; he wore it almost everywhere—to the fields, to school, to meet his cousins, to the playground, and even on later visits to the mela. When he put on his red nose and made faces, passers-by smiled, and friends and relatives laughed and ruffled his hair. Watching people respond to him made him want to entertain them all the time.

The desire to perform grew in the years that followed. He would gather friends and siblings to enact skits for the village elders on special occasions. Bindu bhaiya would be cast as the sarpanch or as an old man because his voice had broken and it made him sound older.

But when two years of poor monsoons had brought Baba to his knees, bhaiya had taken over the responsibilities of the household almost overnight.

It had taken many days to convince bhaiya to let him go to Mumbai, and he had to promise that he would earn an honest living. Dabloo made good on his promise without borrowing a single paisa from bhaiya.

When he had finally signed his first feature film two years ago, he sent money and gifts to his family for Diwali. It was a big celebration in the Yadav household that year—their son, who had been cast as the main lead in the movie Ghummakad,[20] was going to be a star. His success felt sweeter because the movie offer had come right after his lowest phase.

Before he had gotten the movie offer, he could not afford a single meal though he worked as a night watchman at a building complex in Bandra, and so he ate langar at the Gurudwara. The security company that had hired him paid poorly and at irregular intervals.

Once, while ambling along Bandstand, he came upon the golden man. The artist was spray-painted from head to toe in golden paint and stood like a statue. Dabloo became that kid at the mela again. He watched the golden man move with such grace that he pulled out a five-rupee coin from his pocket and placed it in the performer's hat. It reinforced a lesson he had learned on the sets of the no-smoking PSA—an artist plays all roles without prejudice. But who was going to give him any roles to play, and when?

Almost as an answer, he received a call the same night. He had to play a clown at the birthday party of a superstar actor's child. The pay was good and he had a week to prepare. He agreed, more determined than ever to turn the tide of his fortunes.

While on guard duty, Dabloo, unlike the other two guards, preferred walking around the building to keep himself awake. But they jumped up when they heard the thump of Dhananjay Nanda's walking

---

[20] Wanderer or nomad.

stick. The yesteryear film-maker, the building's most famous resident, had recently returned after medical treatment in America and looked even frailer than he had before. This was the third night he'd stepped out so late for a stroll. His attendant told Dabloo later that it was because of his jet lag. His irregular sleep cycles notwithstanding, Dhananjay Nanda liked making conversation with the staff. If the old man called on any of them, they were happy to accompany him on his walk.

'Dabloo, what are you doing these days, besides wasting your time as a watchman?'

He laughed. 'Sir, I go for auditions, and work a day shift as a film crew whenever a shoot happens.'

The old man stopped to look at him. 'Do you have a wife?'

Dabloo's cheeks turned pink. 'No, sir.'

'Good, otherwise she would have left you with that busy schedule of yours.' He resumed his walk. 'When I was your age, I used to work nineteen hours a day. It's a surprise my wife did not leave me. But now, even when we have computers and everyone is better connected, see how many couples are getting divorced.' His eyes were glazed and he seemed lost in thought.

Dabloo wondered if the old man was referring to his film-maker son, Arjun Nanda's failed marriage. The news had made a splash in the papers, bringing the media to the building. The watchmen had had a tough time keeping the reporters at bay and pushing back the mics and cameras they kept thrusting through the grill.

'*Children are very important people. In my time,
I used to show the rushes*[21] *of some of my films to my
children first—if they liked it, I would keep it. Their
responses are the most genuine. That's why I say, if
you can entertain a five-year-old, then you can rule the
world of entertainment,*' said Dhananjay Nanda. '*You
must watch* Mera Naam Joker, *the movie made by my
dear friend, Raj Kapoor. He acted in it too and played
the role of a clown. What a classic!*'

Dabloo's performance at the birthday party had
been a hit. The kids had screamed for more, while their
nannies fed them cake and other treats. He juggled to
the beat of the music, mixing it with pantomime, which
drew more laughs and claps. But it was his pied-piper
act that had sent the audience into a frenzy—after he
played dead, he had jumped to his feet, letting the kids
chase him, before falling '*dead*' again. He had been in
the middle of his act when he noticed the wallet fall out
of Dhananjay Nanda's pocket as he got up to leave the
party. In a flash, Dabloo had picked it up and returned
it to the old man.

Dhananjay Nanda's eyes had bore into him. '*What's
your name?*'

'*Dabloo, the watchman,*' he said, scuttling away as
soon as the kids were about to catch up with him.

The next day, Dhananjay Nanda summoned
Dabloo to the penthouse and gave him a slip of paper.
'*This contains the telephone number and address of*

---

[21] Raw footage of films.

Mickey Taneja. Call and then meet him. Tell him you will work in his movies as per my orders.'

'Why take random favours from people in the industry, Papa?' Arjun Nanda spoke as he strode into the living room, not realizing that Dabloo, though about to leave the house, was still within earshot.

His father's voice was stern. 'You launch so many useless people; if I want to help out a sincere artist, I will. I saw him perform yesterday—he's talented and more importantly, he doesn't steal. He's earning with dignity, something more well-known artists should learn to do.'

'How do you know he can act?'

'I don't know. That's why I sent him to a casting director and not a film-maker. My job was to recommend him to somebody resourceful. If the boy is good, he will find his stage.'

For Dabloo, to go back to the casting office to meet 'the' Mickey Taneja was itself an achievement. He was signed up to play the protagonist, a thief, in the comedic feature film, Ghummakad. It was his first shoot as a primary character, with his own make-up and costume attendants, and his personal vanity van. He touched the ground of the set as one would at a place of worship when one of the spot boys, Mangat, brought him the coconut prasad.

But his joy was short-lived. The movie's release stalled because of a clash between the producer and distributor. Just when he'd begun to feel that life was coming full circle, it had brought him back to square one.

Dabloo watches the waves rise higher when suddenly, he feels a sharp pain in his back. He turns to see a cop holding a lathi. 'Don't you know it's a complete lockdown? What are you doing loitering on the beach?'

He jumps to his feet and runs for his bicycle, pedalling fast to escape a blow from another cop who is closing in on him.

* * *

'I doubt Ruchi will be of help,' Aditi says after Meera tells her about their conversation.

'I think so too. On another note, Lisa called, the talent agent I met at the grocery store. I'm shooting for a print ad for Be-positive pregnancy test kit. If that's not irony, I don't know what is. I have to look like an expecting mother—stuff a cushion under my clothes.'

'How are you going to shoot it?'

'The team will instruct me on a video call. I'll show them my house, they'll select a spot, tell me the angles and poses, and I'll click my pictures accordingly. Sounds easy but it's a full day's work.'

'So much for getting into the skin of the character!'

Meera laughs. 'I'm lucky to get a paid gig, however small, even as I run the risk of getting fired from my major paid gig.' Her heart skips a beat at the thought of losing her role in *Bowled Over* but she cannot let herself think about it, or she'll lose her bearings completely. 'Besides, I already signed up with Lisa's agency so might as well have a go at it.' Meera's phone shows a notification.

'What's the commission like?'

'She has charged me a sign-up fee, actually.'

'How stupid can you get, Meera? Nobody charges to give you work. Even someone like me knows that!'

'She's got me a project; how can that be bad?'

'How much did you pay her?'

'Rs 3500 after the Covid-19 discount.'

'Why don't I send you my bank details too?' Aditi cannot disguise her anger.

'Relax, the print ad is decent money.' She checks the message that has just come through.

'Ruchi has shared the phone number of a gynaecologist—Manoj Mathur.'

Take #14

Abort Mission

The doorbell has rung a few times. Meera can feel fear spread its tentacles over her body. She has been standing motionless just a few steps shy of the main door, contemplating if she should open it at all and allow a male gynaecologist to examine her. Dr Manoj Mathur hadn't answered his phone the previous day, choosing only to send messages on WhatsApp. His display picture is a motivational quote that hadn't inspired any confidence in her either. Had it not been for the pandemic, she would never have let a medical practitioner she hasn't even spoken to anywhere near her, especially when alone at home—questionable male gaze aside, what if some complications arose during the abortion or because of it and there was no one to help? But the being incubating inside her womb is a terrifying reality, much more terrifying than all those probabilities or even the possibility of catching the virus. The doctor assured her that he would abort the foetus and confirmed an appointment for today. Feeling at her wit's end as far as her options were concerned, Meera had finally shared her address without further thought.

The doorbell rings yet again. Face fully wrapped with her scarf, she turns the knob with sweaty palms, and peers through the tiny space that the safety chain allows.

'Shilpa? I am Dr Manoj Mathur.' The hoarse, muffled voice emanates from a woman's body. Clad in a loose salwar suit, holding a worn-out black bag, with a small purse hanging from one shoulder, her orange hennaed hair fades into grey strands near here temples. The woman must be in her mid-fifties. Her face is hidden behind her mask, but her hazel eyes gaze steadily at Meera, who is relieved to see a lady doctor.

'Yes, I am Shilpa. Please come in.'

Adopting a false name for the abortion procedure felt natural. Her situation is traumatizing enough as it is; she didn't want to deal with stigma about her sexual and reproductive choices. If uncomfortable questions come up, she will manufacture a husband who is either dead or locked down in another city because he was travelling. *Oh, but what if the doctor asks to see an identity card as proof for medical records?* Meera sprays half a bottle of sanitizer on the visitor, almost soaking her in it.

'Please take off your scarf, dear,' says Manoj. 'And also, your bloomers.'

Meera can't believe she's heard correctly. Who uses the word bloomers these days unless they're studying history? If her speech is so old-fashioned, how outdated is her equipment and how obsolete are her methods?

'Aren't you the girl from that SWIM dishwash detergent commercial?' Dr Manoj looks keenly at her once she removes the scarf.

In her head, Meera swears but outwardly denies the suggestion.

'You look very similar to the girl in that ad. Have you seen it?' She pulls Meera's lower eyelids to check her haemoglobin.

Meera wonders if the doctor can spot her annoyance too.

'I need to examine your pelvic area, dear. Please bend your knees and open your legs wide.' The doctor presses around her vulva and squints her eyes to look closely at it as if she's going to find the foetus waving back at her. She examines her for a while longer before pulling off her gloves. 'When was your last period?'

'31st January.'

'And do you remember the date you had intercourse last?'

'It was 14th February.'

Dr Manoj counts the weeks passed on her fingers. 'So, you're in the thirteenth week now. Did you not consider taking the medical termination of pregnancy

(MTP) kit?' She presses around Meera's breasts and stomach.

'I read extensively about those abortion pills and their side effects and didn't want to self-administer for fear something might go wrong.'

'Do you live alone?'

'Ye-yes, my husband was travelling for work and got stuck because of the lockdown. What is the procedure for the abortion?' She's irritated, and to make it worse, the room is suddenly baking.

'Must be hard managing all by yourself in this condition, dear. When did you know that you're pregnant?'

'A few hours before the lockdown was announced, I felt nauseated and fainted. I suspected something was wrong, so I took the test, and it came positive.'

'Didn't you suspect it when you missed your period?'

'My periods are irregular—sometimes they can be delayed by a month or more, or I might have to endure three cycles in a span of four weeks. That's why I wasn't alarmed.'

'Did you take a contraceptive pill right after your intercourse?'

'No, we used protection.'

'When did you start to put on weight?'

'I gained 2 kilos in the last two and a half weeks since the lockdown began. Before that, my belly *looked* flat and I did not sense anything unusual. I thought the minor aches and pains were because of heavy exercises or that my PMS was causing bloating.'

Meera feels a bead of sweat trickle down the side of her waist. She's ready to strip off her dress too. As soon as this procedure is done, she's going to take a cold shower.

'Shilpa, the foetus inside you is the size of an apple, a little bigger than a fist.' The doctor makes a fist to demonstrate. 'Usually, one is advised to take pills before the pregnancy has advanced to eight to twelve weeks. But since you are in your thirteenth week, we will have to adopt other measures.' She pulls out a small cylindrical instrument from her bag.

'What's this?' Meera wipes the sides of her face with the sleeve of her dress.

'This is a laminaria.[22] Clinics and hospitals use other devices, but they are bulky and not portable.'

'How does this work?'

'I will insert this spongy stick in your cervix and leave it in for twenty-four hours. It will absorb all the fluid in the surrounding tissue and expand in size, causing your cervix to open. This will induce bleeding, causing everything in your uterus to come out, including the foetus, which will also fall out. It's simple.'

Meera scoffs at the word 'simple'. 'So you're saying this is a *two-day* ordeal?'

'Yes, dear, I will visit tomorrow as well to check on your health.'

---

[22] A small rod of dehydrated seaweed that when inserted in the cervix, rehydrates, absorbing the water from the surrounding tissue in the woman's body. Laminaria expands up to ten times its original size, slowly opening the cervix, and when removed, creates easier access to the uterus.

'My health? What could go wrong?' She feels her throat go dry.

'There are some side effects such as extreme cramping and bleeding—'

'Any complications that can arise?' Meera downs a glass of water as she watches the doctor take her time to answer the question.

'There is a risk of infection if some part of the foetus remains inside. But this is the best we can do given the circumstances.'

'Or else?'

'Or you can choose to have the baby.' Dr Manoj shrugs. 'The decision is yours.'

More sweat trickles down her waist soaking the inside of her dress. Meera opens the window and leans outside, hoping the breeze can cool her. April has been unusually pleasant this year. But ever since she found out she was pregnant, she has been experiencing hot flashes and mood swings. She's afraid these hormonal changes are amplifying her anxiety too.

Whether she has the abortion or not, she's damned. And who knows when a hospital or clinic would be able to come through for her? She has already run out of options; maybe this procedure won't be as bad as it sounds. After all, she has built both strength and immunity with a good diet and exercise in the past few months. She lets out a tentative breath before announcing her decision.

'Let's do this before I change my mind.'

Dr Manoj pulls on fresh gloves as Meera lies back on the sofa.

'Don't worry, Shilpa. I have been practising for over thirty-two years. I've delivered thousands of babies and performed thousands of abortions, both equally successfully. I helped a woman through a complicated labour to deliver a healthy baby, and she was so grateful that she continues to send me a box of barfis[23] on her son's birthday, and he's fourteen years old now. Relax, you're in safe hands.'

'How will I know if the abortion is incomplete, if there's still something left in my body?'

'Usually, one checks that with an ultrasound machine. Since we don't have one, you'll have to wait until the lockdown ends to see a gynaecologist,' says Dr Manoj as she opens a box.

'I can visit you, right? I'm sure you have one at your clinic.'

'No, I don't.'

'Why not?'

'Because I'm a midwife, dear. Ruchi must have told you this already. My clients treat me with so much respect, they call me doctor dai. So, I also began calling myself a doctor the day I bought myself a stethoscope,' she says with a broad smile.

Meera feels her breath stop. 'Wait, aren't you a qualified doctor?'

'Thirty-two years is a long time, dear,' says the false doctor, moving the algae stick towards Meera's body.

---

[23] A milk-based sweet from the Indian subcontinent with a fudge-like consistency.

The words are meant to be reassuring but Meera cannot trust this quack. She screams the first word that comes to mind, 'Abort!'

'I am aborting, dear.'

'Abort the *abortion*! I'm sorry, I can't do this. Please leave.'

Take #15

Food Belly

Meera is wrung out. It's been two weeks since the abortion fiasco and the reality of her pregnancy is weighing her down. To make matters worse, the lockdown has been extended by another month and she's still unable to get an appointment with a doctor, which means her earliest hope for an abortion is the end of June. Not only will it be risky by then or even impossible, but with the way things are going, there's no guarantee that the lockdown won't be extended further. She has already reached out to all her contacts, including Divya, her friend in theatre, who seemed to know everyone in and around Aram Nagar, if not all the suburbs of Mumbai.

Divya had said: 'I spoke to my friend's aunt who's a dermatologist in Hyderabad, but I wish I could do more. Let's hope she can connect me to a gynaecologist in Mumbai. I'll pass on the number once I get it. Hang in there, okay?'

The constant worry has caused Meera more exhaustion than her physical condition. Sometimes, she just languishes by the window considering her situation. She had envisioned a shining career in the movies, bright as the rays of the sun reflected off the glass of the building in the distance. Winning the role in *Bowled Over* had given form to that vision. She had been so beside herself with joy while signing her contract that she had to pinch herself to believe it was real. And then, in the snap of a finger, everything crashed at her feet.

The setting sun makes a perfect circle and reminds Meera of a pregnant, full-grown belly. To distract herself, she jumps to her feet and looks for something to do. Some days, she would deep clean the house until she dropped, or snack mindlessly as she scrolled through YouTube or read fragments from books, not watching or reading anything through. So, when Divya had mentioned a workshop-cum-rehearsal that would culminate in an online play, Meera had asked if she could participate. She would only be paid a token amount but she was willing to take anything that would take her mind off her situation.

She is playing the role of a lawyer fighting on behalf of the teenage son of wealthy parents in a hit-and-run case. She is 'the devil's advocate'. For the Zoom calls, she wears Raghu's T-shirts because they are loose and act as the perfect cover-up. Once, a team member had joked about her fashion statement to which she said spontaneously, 'Let's just say boyfriend-tees are the best way to hide a food belly.' Her straight-faced comment had raised some laughs but she herself had found no humour in it. She was at her wits' end. *How long could this excuse last?*

Meera watches the sky burst into shades of reds and yellows as the sun goes down behind the building. On days like these, Patti's words would come through like an omniscient narrator in a play—*time remedies everything, chellam.* But Meera is beginning to wonder if there is a remedy for time. She has managed to keep the news of her pregnancy hidden from Patti who's constantly checking on Meera's well-being, lest it add to her woes; even so much as a sneeze leads to a full-blown interrogation from Patti's end. Meera wonders how she'd react to this piece of information. When the doorbell rings, she realizes she's been sitting still for hours, ever since the rehearsal ended.

It's the watchman. 'Aditi Ma'am asked me to check on you. She's been trying to reach you for the past four hours.'

'I just saw your missed calls and texts, Aditi. I'd turned my phone on silent during the rehearsal and forgot about it.'

'You gave me a fright there, Meeru. I understand you want some space but please don't forget to check your phone occasionally. Or drop me a message so I know you are fine. Just don't go missing-in-action (MIA) unless you're dealing with that ex-boyfriend of yours—*Rogue-hu!*'

'Don't bring him up.'

'Why not? He is a rogue, especially after what he did to you. It was utterly irresponsible of him, and I'm sorry that you have to go through this. But let it be the last time you're suffering because of a fool. Are you listening to me . . . Meera?'

'Yes.'

'Then repeat what I just said.'

'Listen, Ads, I'm not in the mood. I'll talk to you later.'

Meera has been numb since her last conversation with Raghu. She still hasn't been able to process his slip of the tongue. She has begun to keep her phone on silent mode, either forgetting to check notifications or scrolling through them indifferently.

'Is marriage all you can think about right now, Raghu? Do you think that's any consolation? We're in a pandemic and I'm all alone. I have a dozen other things on my mind right now,' she had said.

'Like what?'

'I can't believe your arrogance—all my efforts for an abortion are coming to nought, my career is at stake . . .'

'Your career is all you can think about, Meera. You've become so crabby. What's gotten into you?'

'Your godforsaken sperm has gotten into me! And I'm left to deal with this unwanted pregnancy all by myself! My hormones are out of whack, I can't sleep at night, my legs ache, and I'm constantly fatigued. Want more?'

Raghu uttered a grunt, which made her even angrier. 'Is that the only response you can make? You're such a jerk!'

'Maybe I should've worn a condom that night. At least I wouldn't have to listen to you sounding like a jerk,' Raghu mumbled.

'Did you just say . . . you did not use protection?' Meera choked.

His words rang in her ears, and there was no mistaking the acid tone in his voice. Suddenly, it seemed like she didn't know the person on the other end of the line. Raghu's voice was drowned out by the faint ringing in her ears. She sat down out of a feeling of weakness in her body and stayed in stunned silence for what felt like eternity before drawing in breath to speak again.

'How could you put me in harm's way when you knew fully well that I was too drunk to think straight?'

'Listen, baby, calm down for a minute. All I'm saying is maybe this is a sign for us to be together . . .'

'I'm not looking for any more signs to be with you.' She swallowed before saying the next few words.

'This is the end of the road for us. And I promise you won't be hearing from me, let alone hearing me sound like a jerk.' Meera was surprised at the frigidness in her own tone as if a decision had been made for her and she was merely the messenger.

Thinking about that conversation now makes her see red. How could a man she'd loved with all her heart, whom she'd vowed to spend the rest of her life with, suddenly seem so repulsive? He was the same person who brought her chocolates to pep her up when she was bogged down by period pain, showered her with surprises and thoughtful gestures like bringing her yellow lilies when she'd never mentioned they were her favourite flowers. For someone so tuned in to her likes and preferences, it was disappointing that he was unable to see her most obvious desire to choose an acting career over a regular desk job. But even that was a difference of opinion she was willing to handle. That he would act so irresponsibly to jeopardize her career and above all, her health, is what feels like a slap to the face—one that sets her head spinning. *When did the acts of affection become affectations?* Just thinking about Raghu confuses and angers her. His betrayal has thrown her off balance.

Meera wakes up the next day too worn out to cook and decides to order food online. She's still on her staple diet of poha and nimbu paani, the only food she can keep down. Hopefully, she'll feel better before rehearsal begins in two hours. When the phone rings, she hopes it's the delivery boy, but it's Patti. The only time Meera has heard Patti sound this sombre is when she's talking about Appa.

'You sound as if you've lost a bet to Shashi Attai. What's the matter?'

'Raghu called.'

Meera ignores the delivery boy's call beeping in the background and waits for Patti to say more.

'First, he complained that you had blocked him. I told him you must have had your reasons. When he realized I wouldn't connect him to you, he told me about your condition.'

'What did you say?' Meera presses her forehead to ease the dull, squeezing pain.

'I told him that if I were you, I would have blocked him too. I wish I could be with you right now, chellam. I feel so helpless,' Patti says, between sniffles. 'I wish I had said this to Revathi when she was expecting you and Vinod was having drunken outbursts all the time. But I'm telling you now. You cannot sit in the snow and hope to stay warm by burning a few matches. You'll have to light a fire strong enough to heat you. Let everything you're feeling and experiencing power you through this journey. Use it as a torch to find your way out of the woods. Don't give up on yourself. Do everything you can to survive.'

Meera feels a pang in her heart. The truth is, Amma gave up on herself. She had channelled her grief through her writing until she could no longer bear it and took her own life. Meera was four when Amma died, but to date, Patti doesn't make a direct reference to her death, choosing to talk in metaphors.

'What if I caused a forest fire with that burning torch, Patti?' she says, trying to lighten the mood in spite of the lump in her throat.

'At least you won't need a torch to show you the way out, chellam.'

They both laugh even as tears roll down their faces. In that moment, everything is well.

Meera remembers her food order only when the bell rings. As she picks up the parcel at the doorstep, someone calls her name. It seems to be the young, scrawny delivery boy standing near the staircase. He removes his mask for a moment and she recognizes him.

'Dabloo?'

'I saw your profile on the app, so I thought I'd come see how you are. One hardly sees any familiar faces these days.'

'Are you doing well?'

'Yes, ma'am. Initially, I was worried about money. But after a few days, I thought there is no point in feeling sorry for myself, so I began looking for a job. Luckily, a friend helped me get this job. I'm doing what I did on set—serving people.'

'That's a positive attitude to have. How many orders do you deliver in a day?'

'Average forty-five to fifty.'

'That's a lot of contact even for contactless deliveries.'

'That is why we must follow safety guidelines very strictly. But today is a slow day. This is my first delivery. I think more people are choosing home-cooked meals now.'

'I prefer home food too, but I ran out of groceries. Now that you mention it, do you know someone who would deliver home-cooked meals?'

'I don't know anyone, ma'am, but I can ask and tell you if you give me your number. And you can take mine in case you need anything. I live close by, in Versova village.'

It's only afternoon when Meera finishes rehearsals, but it seems like the entire day is gone. Patti's words play on a loop in her head as she looks out the window. Patti's right; she should stop feeling sorry for herself and focus on finding her bearings. Even Dabloo, who has far fewer resources, is getting on with his life. But right now, making a livelihood will have to align with her immediate priorities of health and peace. She cannot keep climbing up a downward escalator any more.

All her life, she had been determined to not become her parents. Yet she had gone about mistaking romantic gestures for love and choosing a partner who, on many occasions, had reminded her of Appa. By enabling Raghu's behaviour, she'd sabotaged her own peace of mind. But she's determined to break this pattern of behaviour. Lest she pass it down to her baby.

Wait, did she just use the word 'baby' for what's growing inside her? Is she losing hope with getting an abortion or is some part of her mind already beginning to accept the reality of her becoming a mother? Unexpectedly, she remembers a day from the shoot of *Bowled Over*—in a scene showcasing the coin toss before a cricket match, her character Naintara watches the umpire flip the coin, certain of her decision. But now, at this very moment in her life and before the *coin touches the ground*, as Meera, she is leaning towards the possibility of motherhood. This transition is so sudden that a chill runs through her body.

Meera is no longer gazing wistfully outside the window; she's staring, focused on the arc of every bird's flight, the soft howl of the sea wind and the rustle of the leaves on trees; her senses are heightened with this new-found awareness. Even the building which tucks the sun behind it cannot hide the spectacle of colours the light creates in the sky. It feels symbolic: the sun may be setting on her career, but maybe she needs to see it as letting her old self die for the new to be born.

Take #16

Who Is She?

The ticker tape on the news channel shows the growing numbers of infections and deaths due to Covid-19 as Mickey reads Reshma's resignation email. Her email reeks of resentment; she has spared no words in declaring herself as the engine behind the machine without whom his casting agency would sputter to a complete and final halt. It's a good thing she has marked two colleagues and human resources (HR) on the email. Her sanity is laid open to question without him even having to prove the point. He looks at the news. The anchor is debating the global impact of Covid-19 with a local politician who is bent on pinning the responsibility of the crisis on his opponent. When Anamika calls, he mutes the TV.

'Had I known you were about to get on a work call with Reshma right after I messaged you, I would have told you to approach her with tact. What was the need to shoot your mouth off at her?'

'I was furious, Anamika. She can't do this to me—I have shown her the ropes, given her opportunities to grow and mentored her. Before walking into my office, she had worked as an AD on a regional film and as a creative associate on a TV show but knew zilch about casting. I thought she'd be one of those job-hoppers but when she gave me a sob story about her financial condition, I hired her on compassionate grounds. She stayed nine years in the company, which means I must have done something right. And this is how she repays me?'

'I repeat, Mickey, tact is what you should have used instead of going all guns blazing at her without proof. All I said was, Reshma is a friend of the #MeToo accuser. That does not make her guilty—'

'Then why did she resign?'

'You must have said something severe.'

'I say things all the time! She never had a problem earlier. Why now?'

'Maybe, this was the straw that broke the camel's back.'

Everybody at the office knew how close Reshma and Mickey were; she was even called Mickey's work-wife. Anamika wonders if Mickey knew the gossip that went on behind his back. The #MeToo movement may have made Reshma see something that had happened between Mickey and her in the past with new eyes. Anamika secretly admires Reshma for having had the courage to retaliate if she is, in fact, the accuser.

It's time exploitative people like him meet their match in their protégés.

Mickey wonders when his spate of bad luck is going to end. As if the allegation and ASN fiasco haven't been rough enough, he now has to cope with Reshma's treachery as well.

He feels the walls closing in on him. A walk will solve that—not only is it good for his diabetes but he'll get some fresh air as well since the streets are free of traffic and the pollution levels have come down. But the best part will be not being hounded by the public. This is the real blessing of the lockdown: until now, he could never have imagined walking freely on the streets of Mumbai.

He strolls past the neighbourhood grocery store, where someone is drawing circles spaced far apart on the ground with chalk. It's funny how people cross the line in spite of being told to stay within the boundaries. It's as if they are testing the limits for the next time they want to push them. It reminds him of the first time Reshma came on to him.

'It's pretty late. What are you doing in the office when everybody is at your colleague's farewell dinner?' he had said.

Reshma had played with her hair before she answered. 'She's your colleague too, but here you are, working all by yourself.'

'I would have gone had it been a private lounge or a house party, but everyone wanted to go dancing. You know how I feel about . . .'

'Feel about what?' She swivelled in her chair, turning to face him.

'Public appearances . . .' Mickey was no stranger to sexual signals from eager women. He wondered if he had missed any cues from Reshma earlier. She did seem vulnerable after her engagement had been broken off. If she was looking for a casual fling to cope with her grief, he was willing to step in.

He had responded, after which she began to blow hot and cold to his advances. But he didn't think she was being a tease; it was like she was swinging on the pendulum of her emotions. He should have noticed her unstable tendencies the first time she lost her temper with the actors during an audition, and he should have fired her then for misconduct. In the three years since then, he'd been playing he knew not what game, till she had kicked him in the balls with the false allegation.

Mickey is almost back home when the watchman of a neighbouring building stops him. Jolted back to the present, he focuses and sees two full-grown leopards pawing each other playfully in front of his building.

The watchman says, 'I saw the leopards coming this way and immediately informed the society president. The animal rescue team is on their way and no one can enter till they arrive. Please come in here, sir.'

'But where did they come from?'

'Who knows, sir? The society president thinks they could have strayed from the forest area. The fence around the reserve must be broken somewhere, and there are no people to mend it now. There is no traffic also, so the animals must have escaped and come here.'

Mickey stubs out his cigarette, cursing his luck. What are the odds of being caught in a bizarre circumstance just when he urgently needs to use the washroom?

As he enters the residential complex, a stranger approaches him. 'What a surprise, sir! I didn't know we were neighbours. Do you live in this building?'

Mickey doesn't recognize the Johnny Bravo clone who is extending an arm for a handshake. Mickey greets him with a namaste. He looks at the leopards again, nestled comfortably right outside the gates of his building and showing no intention of leaving any time soon.

'I am Jayesh, an actor. I've seen you many times but never had the opportunity to meet you.'

Mickey is never one to miss an opportunity. This man will be his ticket to a washroom. As they ride up the elevator in silence, Jayesh thanks his stars. The king of the casting jungle himself has walked into his territory. He would love to say something witty but he cannot find the right words. He shows Mickey the facilities, using the time to figure out how to make a strong impression on him when he emerges.

Mickey kills time in the washroom—anything to avoid the energy bunny outside.

Jayesh paces: he must talk about his 87,516 fans on TikTok because big numbers mean business, visibility, brand partnerships, film roles and TV commercial offers. At the rate he's growing, he'll soon reach half a million and then a million followers. He has become the hero of many couch potatoes looking for distraction and entertainment during the lockdown.

When Mickey comes out, Jayesh waxes eloquently about his love for acting and the film-makers and performances that inspire him but Mickey cuts him short.

'What is your pain point? What makes it difficult for you to sleep at night?'

Jayesh is quiet, thinking, and Mickey turns to leave. But he can't escape so easily.

'What you just said, sir—how is that related to my passion for acting?'

'Emotion is one of the most potent tools for an actor. Think about what bothers you the most about yourself and others, or what breaks your heart. Spend as much time as you can watching people instead of staring at your screen. Real actors aren't made on social media—they are a sum of their observations and experiences in real time.'

Jayesh stands still. He has been through bouts of sadness because of Zainab. Surely that will show in a performance, provided his role has the scope for that emotion. He asks, 'Are you casting for any projects? Could I send my profile to you?'

Mickey sighs. The number of actors who spammed him was higher than Jayesh's social media followers. 'Email me your profile and number and my office will contact you if something comes up.'

'Thank you for sharing your email and for the acting advice.'

'It's more a life lesson, kid. For acting advice, I suggest you invest in an acting coach or join my online masterclasses.'

As he leaves, Mickey tells himself that the next time around, he'll pick the hungry leopards over the aspiring actor.

* * *

The pregnancy has altered Meera's taste buds. In spite of having cooked herself idli and sambhar, she orders a portion of poha to accompany it. When Dabloo comes to drop off the order, he tells her his plans to start a tiffin service of his own to supplement his salary.

'The lockdown is really making people explore their options. Who would've thought?' Aditi says on the phone, later that evening. 'How're the rehearsals coming along?'

'I'm drifting as if I've lost my emotional range to play this character even though I'm brimming with emotions because of my pregnancy. I think I'll pull out of the play. The rehearsals are too intense and it's already beginning to give me "virtual fatigue".'

'Tell me about it! I'm taking management classes on Zoom, and I swear, I could punch the participants who leave their mics on despite reminders to mute them. But Meera, think before you quit. At least the rehearsals give you something to look forward to in the day.'

Meera feels the cushion curve around her back as she leans against it and rolls her neck in slow circles to ease the stiffness. Of late, due to the changes in her body, she has started to become aware of the smallest sensations of comfort and discomfort. It's funny how pregnancy is making her notice these small things. When she was with Raghu, she almost always ignored the signs her body gave her. She was available round the clock for him, especially when she was in Chennai. Even after a demanding week at work, she would allow him to gobble up most of her weekends, leaving her with barely any time to sleep, let alone to spend at leisure or with Patti. She wonders: *Has the pregnancy been a wake-up call for me?*

Meera looks at her tummy (which looks a tad bigger than the food belly she gets from overeating) and wonders if the life growing inside her can feel what she feels. She'd read an article which said that at fifteen-odd weeks, a baby can use its facial muscles. She feels a sudden urge to look at her baby. She has read about expectant mothers crying at the sight of their ultrasound scans and always thought it an absurd reaction to a black-and-white image of cloudy waves and dots. But now she wells up at the realization that even contacting a gynaecologist would be a miracle, let alone having the opportunity of seeing her baby in the womb. How odd that till just a week ago she was on a mad hunt for a gynaecologist for very different reasons! Maybe it's good she hadn't found anyone earlier.

She lets out a long sigh, gently patting her stomach as if to reassure the little one. Maybe this is how things are meant to happen; maybe in caring for the baby, she will learn how to care for herself. Maybe life will reveal its lessons gradually over time. She may not have all the answers yet but she's growing sure about one thing: Raghu is the mistake, not the baby.

* * *

Jayesh yawns and stretches. He has barely slept in three nights. Mickey's words still echo in his ears. *What bothers you about yourself? Real actors are a sum of their observations and experiences.*

He knew that staying back in Surat would suck him into the family's real estate business but worse, his relatives would insist that he 'settle down'. His chachi[24] had already drawn up a list of eligible girls from the Sindhi matrimony website, and always found a way to bring up the topic, no matter how unrelated the conversation or inappropriate the place. Like the one time they were in the stands watching a nail-biting Wimbledon final between Federer and Nadal, and she opened the profile of a new match on her phone and passed it down the row of relatives to Jayesh asking for his opinion. 'She's a tennis enthusiast too!' she said, loud enough to draw a few irritated looks her way.

But Jayesh had decided by then that he wanted an audience screaming his name just like the fans in the stadium did for their heroes. The problem was that neither was he inclined towards sports nor did he have the musical skills to perform on stage or in videos. Becoming an actor in Bollywood held promise—he

---

[24] Paternal uncle's wife.

believed it wouldn't be long before he would be racking up roles on the strength of his personality alone.

'*How will you contribute to the business if you start acting?*' *Pappa had asked him, voicing everyone's opinion at the dinner table. Luckily, Mummy had made a timely interjection. She had leaned close to Pappa's ear. 'Venus is retrograde in his chart. According to Pandit ji, this will make him spend more money than he earns till the age of thirty-one. So, until then, let him find a job or hobby that pays for his expenses.'*

Pappa was still reluctant but gave in after Jayesh offered to take care of their vacant properties in Mumbai. Nevertheless, he'll still have to prove his success to his family before he proves it to anyone else, which in their books means making ten times more than his expenses for the entire period he's been in Mumbai.

With Covid-19 putting a stop to all physical auditions and limiting offers from big banner film houses, he wonders if being unable to meet his family's expectations could be his pain point.

The sound of glass breaking and people quarrelling sends him to the balcony to investigate. It's his neighbours from the apartment diagonally below his own, the house where the battered woman lives. The noise dies down as abruptly as it erupts. Humans are a strange species; *why do people who are unhappy with each other live together?* He pushes thoughts of Zainab aside and puts his mind on his assignment for the day.

He needs to record an audition for a hand sanitizer ad. As he gets dressed, he thinks about the oddity of time. In the 1970s–80s, television commercials looked like home videos. In 2020, television commercials *are* home videos.

'Our health is in our hands. And no one understands this better than *Hy-Genie* hand sanitizer. Its powerful antibacterial gel is 99.9 per cent effective against germs, and its non-dehydrating formula leaves your hands clean and soft. Also, with every purchase of *Hy-Genie* hand sanitizer, you help someone in need by contributing to the "Hold Someone's Hand" initiative.'

Jayesh is on the fourth take of his audition when he hears someone talking in low tones. He'd forgotten to shut the balcony door earlier; now he'd have to redo the take. Maybe he should request the neighbour for a few minutes of silence? He leans over the railing to say so when he sees the battered woman choking back tears as she speaks on the phone. Maybe he should not make the request.

'The liquor shops are closed. I'm worried that if I don't find any alcohol by tonight, he'll kill me. No, he can't hear me; he's taking a bath. I've stepped out to the balcony to call you.'

Jayesh steps back. Either he can wait until she goes back inside to record once more or he'll send the previous take to the casting agency.

'Could you help me?' The woman's voice is louder. She has seen him; she must have extraordinary peripheral vision. Jayesh leans forward.

'I know it's a crazy question to ask, but do you have any alcohol in your house?'

Jayesh isn't much of a drinker but remembers a bottle of booze left over from a party from what seems like aeons ago.

'Could I have some of it?' she asks, taking his silence for agreement. 'I can come over to get it.'

'No! I mean, I will bring it downstairs. House number seventy-two, right?' It's better for him to drop off the alcohol at her doorstep and vamoose than for her to come over. One never knows—she may overstay her welcome.

'Yes. Can you bring it over immediately?'

<u>L. MANGESHKAR</u>
<u>S. LANDGE</u>
<u>72</u>

The brass lettering is dusty. The door is opened even before he can ring the bell.

'I cannot thank you enough for this,' the woman says, pulling the bottle out of his hand. Her lower lip is bruised and swollen, and fine lines are bunched together around her eyes. Strands of grey hair are pulled into a bun and she's wearing a dupatta over a nightgown. She must have made quick adjustments to her appearance before attending the door. He can't tell if she's someone who has aged naturally or because of stress. Even though she has put on a polite smile, he can see a frown line almost carved between her eyebrows. 'This will buy me at least three to four days.'

'I'm sorry?'

'I meant this bottle will last my husband three or four days.' She looks behind her before continuing in a whisper. 'My husband doesn't like me singing. Before the lockdown, I used to be able to do my *riyaaz*[25] every day when he was at work. But since he has run out of his supply if he so much as hears me humming . . .'

'Why don't you ask for help?'

'What if the media catches wind of it? My family would be embarrassed.'

'Are you related to Lata Mangeshkar?'

The woman lets out a small laugh. 'I wish, but no. The L on the nameplate stands for Lokesh, my husband.'

'Sarita!' The sound wipes the smile from her face. The voice approaches, saying, 'Where is my white shirt? I've told you a hundred times to leave my things exactly where they are. Why are you standing with the door open? Who's outside?'

'Our neighbour from the floor above. He has brought you some vodka.'

An imposing figure with a scraggly salt-and-pepper beard and dark circles under his eyes opens the door wider. He's wearing a vest over track pants and scans Jayesh from head to toe. 'I have seen you making videos sometimes. What's your name? What do you do?'

'Jayesh. I'm an actor and influencer on TikTok. It's part of my job to make content.'

'Please come in for a cup of tea.'

---

[25] Singing practice.

Jayesh refuses the invitation, but his host is having none of it. The hand on his shoulder is forceful, ushering him inside.

'Sarita, find my white shirt but before that, make us some tea.' He turns back to Jayesh with a gleam in his eyes. Lokesh drums his fingers on the coffee table, whistling softly, waiting for his wife to leave before speaking. Sarita, wise to his manoeuvres, lingers, drawing the curtains of the living room fully open. As she fiddles with the ties, Lokesh says, 'Tea, Sarita.'

She asks Jayesh what kind of tea he prefers and walks to the kitchen as if out for a stroll. It's clear she wants to defy Lokesh and be in on the conversation. She's suddenly more at ease than just minutes ago, but this rapid shift in moods makes Jayesh ill at ease. He should never have entertained Sarita's request in the first place, and now he'll have to suffer this drama till tea.

'You've made a fine body! How much do you work out?'

Jayesh knows this question doesn't need privacy, so Lokesh is obviously building up to what he really wants to talk about. Normally, he would be happy to talk about his regimen for hours, but right now, it feels like a chore. Lokesh goes on to ask questions about Jayesh's diet and work but doesn't seem terribly interested in the answers. Jayesh wonders why the man bothered to invite him in in the first place.

Abruptly, Lokesh leans towards him. 'Could you help me? A friend has arranged a few liquor bottles but can't bring them to me. He lives near Nariman Point.

Can you drive me there and back? I'm a pathetic driver or I would have done it myself.'

'There's a curfew,' Jayesh reminds him.

Sarita hums something classical in the kitchen on the other side of the wall. *How could anybody dislike such a melodious voice?* Jayesh wonders. There's a rattle of crockery as she enters with a tray, a broad smile on her face.

'You have a stunning voice. Have you considered playback singing?' Jayesh blurts. He can see Lokesh clench his jaw as he takes a sip of tea.

'I would like to, but I don't know the right people. A friend told me I could start a YouTube channel to reach an audience. But I'm so tech-challenged that I can barely log on to social media, let alone post something. Maybe you can help me? Perhaps, make a video of my song and post it on your TikTok account. Then I'll know if it's even worth going down that road.'

Jayesh darts a look at Lokesh who is adding a shot of vodka to his green tea.

In what seems like an act of rebellion, Sarita sits on the indoor swing, smoothens her hair, clears her throat, and sings something under her breath. She introduces herself on camera and explains that she's invoking the rain gods by singing the '*Megh Malhar*'.[26] This time, her singing is full-throated, and Jayesh is left reeling at her vocal manipulations. It's like listening to a million

---

[26] Malhar is a Hindustani classical raga. 'Megh' means clouds. Legends says that this raga has the power to bring rains in the area where it is sung.

tiny bells tinkling at once. As Sarita's voice fades out, Lokesh replaces his cup noisily on the table. Jayesh would have asked for an encore, but Lokesh looks thunderous so he contents himself with telling her she should seriously consider singing professionally.

She beams at his reaction. 'Show me how to upload a video on TikTok. And could you please share the link with me so I can send it to my friend?' Jayesh does as he's told because she is leaning over his shoulder to watch him upload the video and because he wants to leave as soon as he gets the chance. He wonders about his fans' comments on this post; *what would they think about the company he keeps, no matter how melodious her voice?* He makes a mental note to delete this post shortly after. For now, he can caption it in a way that shows him being a good neighbour, something like—'When the going gets tough, the tough get crooning. #NeighboursGotTalent #LockdownDiaries or 'one cup of tea with a spoon of honeyed voice' #NeighboursThatSingTogether'.

As Jayesh gets up to leave, Lokesh springs to his feet, walking out with Jayesh and closing the door behind them.

'Please drive me to my friend's house. Don't worry about the curfew. I can arrange fake medical IDs for us. You just have to pretend to be a doctor on your way to see a patient, in case we're stopped.'

'I cannot—'

'Why not? You're an actor!'

Just then, Sarita opens the door and tries to pull Lokesh inside. 'He's a neighbour. You can't get him involved. Be thankful he brought you something for now. Jayesh, please leave, otherwise he won't stop badgering you.'

Jayesh's stomach is in knots as he turns to leave. Lokesh seems unpredictable. How will he react once inside? This is what bothers him about people: they can neither live nor let live. Should he stick around and intervene if something goes wrong? Maybe he should ask the watchman to check on them later.

Take #17

Aram Nagariya

In rehearsals earlier today, the play's director asked everyone to talk about their experiences of living through the pandemic. He wanted to include some of the anecdotes in the performance. For most, this would have been a harmless exercise, maybe even a release, but for Meera, the thought of revisiting her circumstances was triggering.

Should she tell them that she found out about her pregnancy on the eve of the lockdown, that it was unexpected and she had failed to get an abortion? Should she tell them about Raghu; that she had broken up with him? Should she mention how she still wrestles with the fear of being ousted from her first feature film? Should she tell them that she is slowly coming to embrace the idea of motherhood?

She didn't talk about any of it. Instead, she shared how her house now looked like an audition room in Aram Nagar. It evoked smiles from everyone, but thankfully, no questions.

Meera isn't hungry but she drags herself to the kitchen to make a sandwich. She needs to move, walk around the house, do some stretches—anything that might dispel the sense of foreboding that has enveloped her. *Is it just her hormones or is something else going on slightly beyond her ability to perceive?* It might be a good idea to distract herself with a movie.

When she comes across the trailer of *Ghummakad*, set to release in less than a week, she rubs her eyes to make sure she's seeing correctly. It stars Dabloo! He plays the role of a thief who befriends a wayfarer, and they set out on the adventure of a lifetime. Does Dabloo know about this? He's been missing and his phone has been unreachable for three days. She knows because she tried to find out if he'd started his catering business so she could order from him. Not only did her call not go through, but the single tick indicates that her message hasn't been delivered either. *Wouldn't his job require him to be accessible during the day at least, or has he changed his number?* She wonders what could have possibly happened to make him go incommunicado.

The afternoon sun is blazing. Oddly, it makes her yearn to walk outdoors. She needs groceries and can visit the supermarket in Aram Nagar for a change instead of the departmental store in her neighbourhood. She sets out, but her relief at walking outdoors is soon obscured by the heat which prickles her skin. She grew up in humid Chennai, but Mumbai's mugginess is unbearable today. Either that or her pregnancy has made her much more sensitive to the heat than she normally is. She should have carried the mini face fan that had been so useful during the outdoor shoots of *Bowled Over.*

Her heart sinks at the thought of the movie again. It reminds her of all she would have to give up for the sake of the new life inside her. How long can she keep news of the baby hidden from the world? Sooner or later, she will have to inform the producers. She should have called them, given in to the impulse when she had it, just like the impulse that had made her step out for this walk with the treacherous sun overhead.

She knows she can't make it back unless she hydrates. There's something perfect for her to drink at the supermarket if only she can remember its name. *I bet Aditi will know.* 'Hey, I'm at the supermarket, cooling myself in the refrigerated aisles. What is the name of that fruit squash you'd bought once?'

Aditi cannot keep the disbelief and concern from her voice. 'Why didn't you send the watchman or someone else to run these errands for you? The heat is unforgiving, and you need to think of your condition now.'

'I just felt like getting some air, but something's not right with you. Why do you sound in such low spirits?'

'I got an email from HR last night saying I've been laid off.'

'Oh no! Does that mean you'll be giving up the apartment here?'

Aditi says she considers it a possibility. Is this the sense of doom Meera has been feeling since morning? It's been agonizing to be all by herself through the pandemic. And now to be stripped of the very hope of her flatmate's return makes her feel uneasy in the pit of her stomach. As she walks back home with her shopping, she gets a sudden cramp which disappears before she's even registered it properly. She feels another one coming on and looks at the empty street. There are no autos or buses in sight, so she'll have to walk home. She picks up her pace, telling herself it's just the heat and her hormones—nothing that a cold shower and a nap won't fix.

Ten minutes later, the trickles of sweat turn into rivulets down her face and she's gasping under her mask. She puts down her bags to catch her breath. As she wipes the rim of her sunglasses, a light breeze blows dust her way. She realizes that she's standing at the entrance to Aram Nagar. The reality of Aram Nagar, traversing its roundabout, rushing from one false-ceilinged studio to another—it feels like it happened a hundred years ago. Almost every structure held a world of promise—be it a casting office, workshop space or production house. Each day came with the challenge of a new audition. And each audition gave her a sense of purpose and movement, so wildly in contrast to her boring desk job in Chennai. What fun it had been to play cricket with the kids the evening she was confirmed for *Bowled Over*! Divya and she had celebrated at Cafe Blue later that evening. But not before she'd made a complete fool of herself in front of Mickey Taneja. Those days, when her worries orbited around acing an important audition, getting into the skin of a character to prepare for a role, or finding decent rental accommodation . . .

A strong gust of wind breaks her absorption and reminds her to get going. As she picks up her bags, cramps shoot through her belly and down her calves. She doesn't know she's screaming, losing her balance. She falls to the ground.

Take #18

Ghummakad

Gudiya's left slipper has separated into two. As she walks, the insole slaps against her foot while the outer sole drags on the dusty tarmac. Her small steps have become even smaller because she's unable to walk without adjusting her slipper every two steps. Dabloo slows down as well—he's been this six-year-old's walking companion the past few days—and watches her struggle with her Bermuda shorts that keep slipping even though her mother had tied a string around her waist to keep them intact. Just then, the thong of her slipper breaks, making it impossible for her to walk any farther. A part of her foot touches the ground and burns her skin. She looks up at Dabloo, squinting because of the overhead sun, and he sees her eyes brim with tears. He places her on his shoulders and picks up her slippers. Holding up the left slipper, he scolds,

'You thief! You stole Gudiya's comfort. You will be punished for this.'

Bending the left slipper in half as if in apology, he whimpers, 'It's not my fault, sir. It is the other slipper's fault. He put too much pressure on me.'

As Dabloo raises the right slipper in protest, the left one begins to thrash it. The slippers fight noisily till one of them slaps Dabloo on the cheek.

Gudiya breaks into giggles and claps. She asks Dabloo for another performance but just then, her mother calls out for her. Dabloo looks in the direction of the voice, trying to locate her among the hundreds of migrant labourers filling his vision, hazy in the mirage created by the scorching June sun.

* * *

A week ago, he'd been surprised to receive a call from Baba; it was usually bhaiya or Ma who called. Baba was sobbing uncontrollably, unable to respond to Dabloo's pleas to tell him what was the matter. Finally, it was Alka didi, his elder sister, who took the phone and told him that Bindu bhaiya was no more.

Dabloo was cycling out of a residential complex after a food delivery when he heard the words, lost his balance out of shock and fell to the ground with his cycle, misaligning its frame and spilling curry from the food cartons. He hurried home, orders forgotten; he needed to get to his village. He pushed aside thoughts of not being able to make it in time for bhaiya's last rites.

He struggled to understand Didi's words as she sobbed. Didi said that Bindu bhaiya had succumbed to a rare type of cancer and she couldn't pronounce the name. Their neighbour's daughter, who had recently completed her MBBS, was visiting her family just before the lockdown was announced. It was she who had pulled some strings and arranged for bhaiya's treatment in the city hospital. But he was already in his last stage of cancer.

'Why did you all hide this from me? I don't live in the village now so I'm an outsider?' Dabloo had yelled despite himself.

'Bindu bhaiya forbade us from breathing a word to you. He made us swear over his dead body.'

Dabloo packed a bag and set off for Kurla station. He would catch one of the Shramik Special trains[27] that were transporting migrant workers and students home during the lockdown. But at the station, even the platforms were choked. It would take hours, maybe days, before he could get close to the train and then into the train itself. He overheard an old man, whom people addressed as Bauji,[28] telling a group of people to try their luck at the next station. The septuagenarian reminded him of his village sarpanch. Standing at about 6 feet, Bauji walked with authority and was accustomed to being respected. He might have been

---

[27] Trains and buses started by the Government of India to move migrant workers, pilgrims, tourists, students and other persons stranded at different places due to lockdown.

[28] Father or fatherly figure.

a wrestler or a police sahib in his younger days. Even though his face looked time-worn, his eyes were bright and alert, and his white, bushy eyebrows made him look stern. If he told you to try your luck at the next station, you'd probably consider it a command rather than a suggestion.

* * *

'Dabloo bhaiya, look, a big fish!' Gudiya points at a bird circling the sky. She moves her head in circles, mimicking the bird's flying pattern.

'That's a hawk, not a fish.'

'Fooled you!' she shrieks with delight. 'Bhaiya, why can't fish fly in the sky?'

'Because God did not give them wings. They are—'

'Wrong! Fish have wings; I have seen it. I had a fish once, Chikki. She died of cholera. When Chikki flapped her feathery wings, she would fly in water. I know it. Fish *do* fly.'

'That's called swimming. Fish swim. Birds fly.' Dabloo corrects her. Fish dying of cholera is new—the child has an imagination.

'Wrong again! Birds swim in the sky and fish fly in water,' Gudiya says between mouthfuls of an overripe apple.

Her steadfast belief in her logic reminds Dabloo of when he was six. *Baba would sometimes sit him on their oxen, Nandi and Sumitra, as they ploughed the field. He always thought Baba and the oxen were simply strolling through the farm till lunch. Bindu bhaiya, seven years older, tried telling Dabloo differently but to no avail. Determined to make his point, bhaiya had once waited till Dabloo was in the field alone and spoke while hiding behind the scarecrow. 'Obey your brother and don't argue with him,' he had said hoarsely, pretending to be the scarecrow come to life.*

Dabloo had jumped in fright till he heard bhaiya squealing with laughter, after which Dabloo chased him across the farm all the way to the marsh, Baba's scolding echoing in his ears long after he had stopped hearing it.

It's cooler now but the night is still, and the air feels sticky against Dabloo's skin. The weather is mimicking his heart—heavy with unshed tears.

The stars look like flecks of talcum powder against the night sky. He's been on the road for a week (he doesn't know how long till he reaches his home town) and his phone is dead. Alka didi must be worried sick because she couldn't get in touch with him. He had told her he was returning home and she had discouraged him; bhaiya would be cremated the following day and he would certainly not have arrived by then. Dabloo squeezes his eyes shut to stop his tears from flowing.

In one of their last conversations, bhaiya had recited the 'Hanuman Chalisa' and extracted a promise from Dabloo, as he had from each member of the family, to recite it every day. Bhaiya knew, perhaps, that even prayers wouldn't save him but at least they would give them the strength to cope with his death. Dabloo wants to scream but doesn't let out a sound. *Why should he keep his promise when bhaiya had hidden his medical condition from him?*

Adjusting his head on the bag he's using as a pillow, he turns sideways. The travelling party of migrants are sprawled across the patch of land. The colour of their skin blends into the night. The quiet is broken only by the sound of crickets and the snores of the sleepers.

An insect bite had irritated Gudiya all day; so much so that she had scratched it till it bled. Yet she continued to scratch the wound. Her mother had washed it with water, rubbed a neem leaf on it and tied a rag around it. 'Tanju bitiya,[29] *she'll recover in no time, just you see,' Bauji had called from the distance.*

Usually, Gudiya would be so tired that she'd be asleep even before somebody set her down, but today, she was cranky and refused to sleep. In trying to distract her, Dabloo had asked her to lie on her back and count the stars she could spot in the sky. She had counted to six and stopped because she didn't know how to count further so he taught her how to count till fifteen, by which time she grew tired and sleepily gestured to her father to carry her. Dayaram coddled her till she dozed off, placed her on the *gamchcha*[30] he had spread under the tree and then lay down beside her.

Dabloo remembers being told that when he was two, he was sick and had a high fever. All home remedies had failed. Nine-year-old Bindu bhaiya had sneaked out of home in the dead of night, walked

---

[29] Daughter.

[30] A traditional, coarse cotton cloth used as a towel or a scarf.

5 kilometres to the local chemist's house and insisted he open his shop so Dabloo could have the medicine he needed. Baba and Ma hadn't even noticed bhaiya was missing until the chemist dropped him off on his scooter at their doorstep. Though just seven years older than Dabloo, Bindu bhaiya was more like a father figure to him. Growing up, he would scold Dabloo and shield him from Baba's wrath with the same fervour.

Dabloo looks up at the stars which seem to be moving across the sky. How he wishes he could stop time, or better still, turn back time and somehow prevent this misfortune. He feels wretched that even though he's walking several hundred kilometres to go back home now, he couldn't do anything when bhaiya was unwell.

A drifting cloud catches Dabloo's attention. Mumbai must be on the brink of monsoon but the city is far behind him. They should reach the border of Madhya Pradesh in another day or so—another state to walk across. *How many miles will he have to walk before he reaches his destination?* Now he is the only son and earning member of the Yadav family; he has very big shoes to fill. His earnings from his jobs in Mumbai will not be enough to provide for his family, even without the additional consideration of his youngest sister's impending wedding. *Does this mean he'll have to take over bhaiya's business in Bettiah?*

* * *

The likes and views on Zainab's Instagram post have skyrocketed in the last three days. The caption reads, 'A sneak peek into the making of the catchiest tune of 2021'. She looks every bit the glamorous showgirl, the tassels on her skirt swinging as she sways her hips. At the sound of 'Cut', she holds her pose, letting the moment stretch before relaxing her shoulders and smiling broadly at someone off-camera.

Jayesh has watched Zainab's video on loop. While she was filming this song, she had barely spoken at home and would go to bed earlier than usual. When asked why she was so quiet, she had blamed long working hours and her exhaustion. She had been cold as ice with him, a complete contrast to her attitude in the video. Had it been the song itself, he would have understood, but this was a behind-the-scenes video, and she seemed so engaged with everyone on the set.

He had asked Bidyut for advice.

'There are plenty of fish in the sea, bro. Get over her. It's common for girls in this industry to lead you on and then ghost you. Never date anyone from the movie business. Take my advice and get back on Tinder. I don't know why you deleted the app when the two of you weren't even exclusive.'

If Zainab wasn't into him, she really had put up a great act. But was it just to freeload from him? Jayesh sighs as he watches her video yet again while putting several heart and fire emojis in the comments.

The doorbell rings, revealing two men in khaki standing a foot away from the door. One of them steps forward, scans the house over Jayesh's shoulder and introduces himself as Inspector Kamal from Versova police station.

'The body of Mr Lokesh Mangeshkar of number seventy-two was found at Versova beach this morning. We are speaking to all those he interacted with over the past few days.' The cop watches Jayesh's eyebrows meet in the middle of his forehead. 'The CCTV camera showed that you visited him yesterday afternoon. Can you tell us the purpose of your meeting?'

The other cop taps his pen on a pad as Jayesh clears his suddenly dry throat before telling them the sequence of events from his visit. It's highly unlikely that he will be charged for passing on a bottle of vodka to an unhinged drunkard he'd met for the first time, yet one could never tell where any investigation might lead. Besides, though he's no expert, Lokesh did not strike him as having suicidal tendencies, but he isn't going to share his opinion with the police.

As they are leaving, the inspector turns back. 'How long have you known Lokesh Mangeshkar's wife?' he asks as an afterthought.

'I met her only yesterday.'

The inspector watches him. 'Are you sure? We believe the husband and wife had a fight soon after you left. According to her, Lokesh was drunk when he left the house. Do you think he could have been upset or threatened by your visit?'

There's an insinuation in the inspector's tone. Does he think that Jayesh is having an affair with Sarita, someone almost two decades his senior? Where do they come up with such ridiculous questions?

'I've already said I don't know either of them.'

'Thank you for your time.'

Jayesh walks up and down the length of his house. There is no telling what the investigation will reveal, but it is unnerving to be questioned. To be caught in someone else's drama and charged falsely is very common these days, especially when it's a high-profile case. But he wonders whether Lokesh also suspected him of having an affair with Sarita. After all, the man had looked at him warily at first before insisting that Jayesh drive him to Nariman Point. What if Lokesh was planning to quiz him about Sarita during the car ride, and based on his answers, 'eliminate' him, have him 'sorted out' by goons or something equally wild? Jayesh shakes his head. Hopefully, it'll be an open-and-shut case of suicide or accidental drowning. Just then, a woman speaks loud enough from the balcony below for her words to be heard clearly.

'I thought she hadn't done her riyaaz in so long because she was still mourning Mai's passing last year. I had no idea she was going through so much. We spoke every week or so and she sounded normal. Sometimes, she would mention an argument with Lokesh or say she was tired because of the housework.' When the woman speaks after a pause, her voice is a couple of notches lower. 'On the day of his death, there was no liquor in the house so Sarita had asked a neighbour for some. How silly of her! Imagine the embarrassment if the news gets out. Apparently, Lokesh was quite drunk when he left the house. He was walking on the beach at high tide last evening. He may have been too drunk to stay upright and the tide carried him away. The post-mortem says he drowned.'

Jayesh has heard enough. Remembering his conversation with Sarita, he types 'Landge music', and Google tells him that in the 1940s, sisters Urmila and Gayatri Landge were well-known classical musicians from Kolhapur, Maharashtra. Sarita must be the granddaughter of one of them. But there's no information about her, and it seems like nobody from the family was ever associated with films. Given Covid-19 and the lack of a Bollywood connection, Jayesh wonders if the media would even cover this incident. At any rate, he'll make sure he stays away from her lest he get drawn into her affairs any further.

The rumble of the skies is followed by a thunderbolt that announces the season's first downpour. As he opens TikTok to capture the rain, a flood of notifications comes through. Sarita's singing video has already amassed 3,00,000 views, likes and comments, and brought in a stream of 23,000 new fans. All within the span of half a day, most of which he has spent sleeping. He smiles. His video is going viral.

Take #19

Solstice of the Soul

The pungent smell of disinfectant hits her nose before Meera opens her eyes. Blurred blue and white figures scramble around, flitting in and out of a swinging door. She blinks a few times to sharpen her vision. The hall is lined with single beds on either side of a central aisle. Where the plastic curtains separating the beds are drawn open, she can see some patients hooked to intravenous fluids while others have oxygen masks on. People in personal protective equipment (PPE) suits with visors in place are going about their duties carrying folders, steel trays and other equipment. It's loud—hospital staff are shouting instructions, patients are moaning and coughing, and announcements are being issued from the intercom, all accompanied by the rhythmic beeping and droning of machines.

She recalls the siren of the ambulance before it halted near her. She was on the ground, unable to move, when the medics lifted her on to a stretcher and into the van. She vaguely remembers being wheeled into this ward and given an injection that made her groggy. She knows something has happened but isn't sure what it is. She needs to ask someone what's going on.

Meera's hand goes to her throbbing right temple. She feels a wound and winces when she touches it. She tries to sit up but a sharp pain in her stomach makes her give up the effort. She calls for a nurse but they are too busy to notice her. The patient next to her breaks into a coughing bout which brings a nurse to him, who pulls the curtains closed, and in minutes, a team of people is in there. Meera can hear fragments of their conversation—something about shifting the patient to the red zone and urgently needing more oxygen cylinders.

Meera looks around, afraid she's surrounded by Covid-19 patients. Why have they put her in this ward? She is sure to get infected, and what would that mean for the baby?

The curtain is pulled back and a doctor checks her pulse. 'How're you feeling?' A nurse clips something to her finger while another straps a blood pressure cuff to her arm.

'What happened?'

'You fainted. You were severely dehydrated when you came in. There was vaginal bleeding as well. You're doing fine, but we cannot keep you here beyond noon tomorrow. Ask someone to pick you up so we can discharge you into their care.'

'But I'm pregnant, at the start of my second trimester. I can't be on my period.'

'I'm sorry, then it looks like you might have had a miscarriage. We'll have to terminate your pregnancy. Call a relative or friend to sign the waiver and we'll discharge you after the procedure.'

'My immediate family and friends aren't in Mumbai.'

'Then you'll have to sign the consent form yourself.'

Before she can ask him anything else, the entire team has moved on.

Much later, a nurse tells her, 'You tested negative for Covid, but antibodies have been detected in your blood.'

'But I didn't feel sick or anything. How is that possible?'

'It happens in some cases; it means you were asymptomatic. With antibodies, you are immune to the virus for at least two to three months.'

'Was the miscarriage because of Covid-19 or the fall?'

'We don't know, but make sure to get a lot of rest.'

'How will I leave the hospital? I don't know anyone in Mumbai who will sign the discharge papers!'

'Are you sure?'

Meera nods, holding back tears.

'Shanta, bed number eight!' someone shouts. The nurse pats Meera's hand and leaves.

Time seems to stand still as Meera looks at the ceiling with its white fluorescent lights, the chaos around her fading into nothingness. She feels as if she's living her nightmare of falling off a building. But instead of crash landing at once, she's tearing through one glass roof after another, and she doesn't know how many more storeys there are left.

To think that that one night of unrestrained drinking with Raghu was all it took to bring her to this point. If only she could go back in time and put the glass down right after she picked it up. Growing up, she had despised Appa drinking and watching him spiral out of control under the influence. She would often pinch her nose closed at the smell of alcohol; the thought of tasting it had never even crossed her mind. What had prompted her to drink after all these years?

Patti was right to warn her against Raghu from the very beginning; Meera wonders how she would react to the miscarriage.

'Aiyo, chellam. I had been feeling a sense of dread for the past two days. Even before you gave me this news, I had decided to walk to Tirupati temple barefoot and do an *angapradakshinam*[31] as soon as possible to pray for you. God knows what ancestral curse we are suffering. It must be even more difficult to manage, especially since you are alone. Can't you call one of your friends from the play rehearsals to help out?'

---

[31] The devotee lies prostrate on the ground with arms outstretched, facing the temple's sanctum sanctorum, and offers prayers to the deity, and then rolls around the temple in the supine position.

'That'd be too much of an imposition. We aren't close enough friends for me to ask them for this favour. Besides, I doubt they'd be willing to risk a visit to the hospital either, let alone care for me through my recovery. Can you hold for a minute?' Meera puts the phone face down on the bed and stretches her arm for the nurse to give her an injection.

Patti says, 'I'm sure someone from my students' alumni network will be willing to help.'

Early the next morning, Aditi calls to say she's had no luck finding anyone either. Propped up against the pillows, Meera wonders how this situation will be resolved. The hospital staff seem to whizz past—and watching them is as tiring as coping with her thoughts. Sitting here quietly, knowing that soon she would be going back to her house, that too without her baby, gives rise to a dull pain in her chest. How will she cope with her loneliness? She longs for a familiar face. If only Patti or Aditi were here. She'd even take Raghu's presence. At least she could fight with him. Anything that would prevent her from feeling like she's on a one-way trip into a black hole.

She's finishing her soup later in the day when she hears a voice she's heard before but cannot place.

'Hello, Shilpa. Remember me?' Strands of hennaed hair are visible under the woman's cap and she's wearing the regulation PPE kit with a mask. 'I am Dr Manoj Mathur.' Manoj looks at her with the same steady, inquisitive gaze as she had when she visited Meera at home.

'Meera, not Shilpa,' Meera says with a smile.

'My friend Shanta works as a nurse here. She told me about you, your miscarriage. She said a patient is alone and needs care. I told her if there's nobody else, I'm willing to nurse them at my house for a few days. I was surprised to see you. I'm sorry you had to go through this. This is a terrible time for a woman to be left alone, no matter how much you like being alone, dear.'

Meera looks at her empty cup. A most unexpected visitor has appeared, willing to take responsibility for her. Manoj was certainly unfit to carry out an abortion, but she must have some qualifications as a caregiver. After all, she's a dai, and Meera needs assistance. Meera says, 'Why don't you come to my house?'

'That won't be possible. I have work and other patients to attend to as well. But you'll be quite comfortable at Devri Chawl. I have a spare room. The tenants left just before the lockdown. Plus, I have briefed some girls from the chawl so they will be there to help you while I'm at work, just in case.'

Feeling depleted and without an option, Meera accepts the offer but decides to take a final call only once she's been discharged from the hospital, and if she doesn't like it at Manoj's, she can always go back to her house. The good thing is that she isn't at risk of contracting Covid, given the antibodies in her system.

* * *

It's as if Devri Chawl is nestled under a different sky. The rooms at the chawl open into a corridor that encloses a rectangular inner courtyard open to the sky. The residents seem to be living in pre-Covid times; there's no trace of social distancing. Children play with marbles in the *wada*[32] under the late afternoon sun. Groups of men and women are collected around the corridor—some are chatting on floor mats, poring over a book, focused on their phones or working embroidery patterns. Some men are huddled over a carrom[33] board. Neighbours greet Manoj and eye Meera as they walk past them and up a flight of stairs.

'I have known some of these people since they were kids. I've helped deliver their babies. That young woman across the verandah had a miscarriage three years ago. I told her not to lose heart because every soul decides when to come into this world. She must take care of her health before taking responsibility for another human. The man next to her is her husband and he's holding their child.' Manoj waves to them before turning to glare at the teenage girl scrolling on her phone. 'Pinky, clean didi's room quickly. She needs to rest.'

Manoj's tenement is across the staircase and Meera will occupy the room next to hers. Her room has an armchair, a cot and a stove, and a clothes line runs across its width.

'I've installed a private toilet and bath which you can use instead of going to the common bathroom.

---

[32] Verandah.

[33] Carrom is a tabletop game of Indian origin, in which players flick discs, attempting to knock them to the corners of the board.

When the lockdown began, I started a Devri Chawl cleanliness campaign. Men, women and children have to clean their living quarters as well as public spaces including the toilets. The family that cleans the best is the winner. The prize is the family's favourite meal cooked for them by their neighbours. It keeps people motivated.'

Manoj brews tulsi leaves, saunf, giloy powder and sugar in a pot of water. 'This *kadha*[34] will improve your immunity; drink it and rest. I have some errands to run. I'll see you in the evening. Let Pinky know if you want anything. Oh, and she told me she has seen you in a TV ad. I told her that that's not you. You just look similar to the actress from it.' Manoj gives her a knowing smile.

In spite of the heat outside, Manoj's room is cool and cosy. Wrapping her fingers around the warm cup, Meera looks out the window. She has known loss through most of her life. Yet, the biggest blow was the loss of agency—of having a pregnancy thrust upon her against her wishes. She'd never thought that she'd be so powerless, her only choice being to put one foot in front of another without knowing where she's headed. The miscarriage is a setback she'll surely overcome with time. But with so much happening so quickly, it feels like she's sitting with her skin peeled off, fearing even the slightest touch.

'Time is a spiral, chellam. We keep returning to the same place till we learn our lessons for good, or till we

---

[34] Decoction.

gain fresh insight into an old situation and break the patterns.'

'I'm back to square one like I was before the lockdown and *Bowled Over*,' she says between sobs.

'I know it's difficult and you can't see the silver lining here. But if it helps, you have a choice now. You are free. You don't have to fend for a child or be weighed down by a partner's demands; you just have to worry about the next audition. Isn't that a different perspective to have?'

Meera composes herself as she sees Manoj approach. 'Manoj ji made the most incredible brinjal dish today. You might want to take down the recipe, Patti; you love brinjal so much. Here, speak to her.'

Manoj steps out into the corridor while talking. When she returns, she says, 'Your grandmother suggested that I listen to the Sri Venkatesa Suprabhatham by M.S. Subbulakshmi every morning to keep negative energies away. I know she meant it for you, so I assured her that you're recovering just fine. I may not have a medical degree but I know my job.' Manoj smiles as she adds diced vegetables to the pan. 'Your grandmother is really protective of you.'

'It has been a rough year so far. To top it off, neither of us can travel, so the situation is making her overly concerned.'

'I forgot to ask you—what about your husband?'

Meera doesn't reply. Pressing the hot-water bottle to her stomach, she remembers how eagerly she had looked forward to her marriage with Raghu, the details she had imagined of their life together and her constant defence of him in the face of Patti's criticism. She shudders at the thought now. 'Boyfriend, not husband. I broke up with him. My unplanned pregnancy was the tipping point.' A sudden wave of calm washes over her. 'Just as I began to accept my pregnancy and welcome motherhood, I had a miscarriage. Isn't it odd?' She speaks more to herself than to Manoj.

'Belief creates biology, dear, on the inside as well as the outside. When I first met you, you wanted an abortion. That intention must have stayed with you long enough to lodge itself as a command to your mind and body. Some thought or emotion must have pushed you over the edge. I'm not saying it's your fault, but there's some truth to our thoughts creating our circumstances.'

'I never saw it like that.' Meera tries to make sense of Manoj's words. Does this mean that she unwittingly brought the pregnancy upon herself too? That would be bizarre. 'I wasn't thinking! The one time he surprised me at my apartment, he brought a cauliflower in the dead of night but not a condom. Was I in denial or was I afraid to confront him because I couldn't bear the thought of losing him?'

'These things happen all the time, dear. I know several women who have gone through similar situations. You will naturally feel responsible, but you must know that the onus of even a single extra moment rests on the man. Unfortunately, a woman pays the price for the man's additional moment of pleasure. Even though you are the wiser for it now, you must know that most men either don't know or don't care because they don't have to go through the ordeal of giving birth. If he loved you, he would have been more responsible.'

* * *

Dabloo has been on the road for almost a month. After fifteen days of walking through Madhya Pradesh, he sees a signpost welcoming them to Jhansi. The walking has taken a toll: his feet are cracked and filled with scabs. He had shoes but days of walking on hot concrete had unravelled their seams. He is wearing the pair of chappals he had fortunately stashed in his bag at the last minute before leaving his house in Mumbai. The blinding light of the sun has baked his skin so much that it is difficult to tell where his skin ends and the tree trunk against which he is resting begins. The heat has even silenced the birds. The summer loo had made two of their group throw up, one of them being Gudiya. She had collapsed, and though she's been revived with sugar water, she still looks sickly.

Bauji sits on his haunches, pressing *khaini*[35] with his right thumb, and says, 'The reporter from the news channel van that passed by the other day said that it'd be better to turn right from the Prayagraj bypass bus stop and catch a Shramik bus, or spend the night at the depot and catch a bus from there the next day rather than walk all the way to Gaya.'

---

[35] A form of chewing tobacco used in India that contains slaked lime.

Dayaram is dozing under the shade of a tree, his head cushioned by the folded gamchcha, while Tanju leans against the trunk, looking vacantly at Gudiya. The rashes all over her daughter's body resemble burns. It's probably what caused the fever that began five nights ago. Gudiya has barely eaten since then, and when Tanju tries to feed her sattu,[36] she pushes her hand away irritably. Gudiya is overcome by a bout of coughing before she stills again in her mother's lap.

Plugging the wad of tobacco into his cheek, Bauji says, 'It must be the evil eye; it cannot be Karona. Even the virus wouldn't be able to withstand this harshness. Bathe her in salt water, bitiya. My daughter-in-law has a packet of salt in her bag. I'll ask her to give you some.'

'Look what I made, Gudiya!' Dabloo holds up a pair of slippers he has made from two plastic bottles that were too flattened to hold water. He had tied the shoelaces from his own torn shoes to make the post and straps for her slippers.

'Fish!' Gudiya's voice is low and raspy but her eyes sparkle at the prospect of being told a story. She extends her arms as if asking Dabloo to carry her.

Dabloo picks her up tenderly and seats her in his lap. She is just a bunch of bones. Holding a slipper in each hand, he says, 'I'll tell you the story of a big fish and a?'

'Small fish.' Both speak together.

He knows she doesn't tire of fish stories, so he begins, using an animated, squeaky tone for the small fish and a deep baritone for the big fish. 'They swim in

---

[36] A type of flour made of gram, pulses and groundnuts.

the cool waters of the ocean near a hot desert island. After playing catch with her friends, the small fish is trying to catch her breath.'

'My fish Chikki used to blow bubbles with her mouth.'

'And that's exactly what the small fish is doing—blowing bubbles. When suddenly, she hears her friends scream, "Watch out for the big fish!" The small fish is quick and slithers away, narrowly escaping the big fish's jaw.'

Dabloo's hands show the big fish slipper chasing the little fish. Gudiya watches wide-eyed till she throws her arms in the air, saying, 'I won't let you eat me, big fish. I can run faster than you. You cannot eat me. Instead, I will eat you!'

She starts coughing again. Dabloo drops the slippers and pats her back. Her mother brings her water to drink and tries to carry her away, but Gudiya resists because she wants to hear the rest of the story.

Dabloo continues. 'Just then, both fish stop midstream as they hear someone singing. It's a melody so beautiful and so magnetic, it draws them to the surface and they see a fisherman in a boat singing aloud to himself:

Between the sand and the sea, there's a wave that rushes to me. In the moments before I'm soaked,

you tell me the secret that makes me choke. Find me where the river meets the ocean,

where the wind blows the sails and the tides turn,

find me where the orange ball of fire rests for the night.

Find me in those waters, and all will be all right.'

Dabloo's voice cracks a little as he hums. Bindu bhaiya sang this song only in his most sombre moments as if humming it gave him hope. He sang it when he was struggling to set up his business and when Baba had fallen seriously ill four years ago. Once, when Dabloo had called him during the lockdown, he had been humming it; his body must have been racked with pain because of the chemotherapy, but he hadn't breathed a word about it. How could Dabloo have become so busy attending to his work that he missed such a vital clue about bhaiya's state of mind? If only he had pressed bhaiya to speak up or spoken to a family member later, he could have somehow sought the help of the producer of *Bowled Over* or even stood outside Dhananjay Nanda's house requesting money for bhaiya's treatment. Even if it was too far-fetched to expect aid, they might have been able to connect him to someone who could have helped.

'Why is the fisherman singing?' Gudiya's voice brings him to the present.

'The fisherman is sad because he is all alone at sea. He doesn't have a friend to talk to or play with, so he's singing to keep himself company.' Gudiya wipes the tear rolling down Dabloo's cheek, thinking it's the character he's playing. 'The big fish is so drawn to the melody that he swims even closer to the boat. As he is singing, the fisherman pulls up the net, trapping the big fish with the other fish. The small fish is agile and manages to slink through the net but the big fish is scared. It tries to wriggle free but fails.'

'Does the small fish help him?'

'Maybe not. She had threatened to eat him, remember?'

'No, I don't like this story ending.' She frowns. 'The small fish has sharp teeth, so she tears the net and because she has a big heart, she releases the big fish. The big fish thanks her and then they become friends.'

'What happens to the lonely fisherman?'

After thinking for a few seconds, she says, 'They become friends with the fisherman too.'

As the sun sets in about two hours, the travellers pick up their belongings and resume their walk towards the bus depot. All except Gudiya, her parents, Bauji, his son and daughter-in-law, and Dabloo.

Gudiya's condition has worsened. Her skin is hot to the touch—as if she's breathing fire. Tanju wipes her forehead with the wet gamchcha while Dayaram looks on forlornly. Dabloo jumps to his feet when Bauji instructs him to bring water from the borewell nearby as they are running short.

Even before he can break into a sprint to fetch it, he hears Bauji reciting the 'Hanuman Chalisa'. When Dabloo had first learnt of how bhaiya had hidden his cancer, he had decided to break his promise in his fury—he would not recite the Chalisa every day. But now, he finds himself joining Bauji in his recitation.

Dabloo is still filling water when a piercing cry rents the air. He runs back carefully, trying to avoid spilling the water. Tanju is shaking the child, who does not seem to respond. Bauji's daughter-in-law rushes to hold Tanju steady, while Dayaram slaps both hands on his head. Bauji squats on the ground near Gudiya's still body.

Her eyes are closed and she looks strangely at peace. Her fingers are wrapped around the slipper, as if she were still in her make-believe world, swimming with the fish.

Dabloo is still staring into space when Bauji asks him to collect wood for her cremation.

Bauji tells the wailing mother, 'If it's *prabhu's*[37] wish, it cannot be averted, bitiya. At least she didn't suffer too long.' His words make Gudiya's mother sob even harder.

Dabloo is relieved to be assigned a task that gives him a chance to step away, to be alone with his emotions. He climbs a tree and applies his full weight to break a thick branch from the trunk. As his grief, anger and helplessness overwhelm him, he feels possessed with the desire to pull down as many branches off the trees by force as he can. He wants to keep doing it till he passes out. As he walks back with the branches, he wonders who must have arranged the wood and *samagri*[38] for bhaiya's cremation, and whether Baba would have been able to light the pyre without breaking down.

Dayaram curses his fate aloud as he and Bauji's son set up the pyre. Bauji utters mantras as Dayaram places

---

[37] God's.
[38] Materials.

Gudiya's body on the pyre and shrouds her body with his gamchcha.

Dabloo picks up the plastic slipper that Dayaram had released from Gudiya's hand. In the little time that Dabloo had known her, Gudiya was staunch in her love for fish, but more than that, in her optimism that all creatures could be friends and live harmoniously. He thinks about putting it next to her on the pyre but tucks it in his back pocket instead.

He wonders about the rest of the journey home without Gudiya for company before he realizes that he should drop the idea of going back to Champaran jilla. Her life could have ended due to anything from exhaustion to infection to even Covid-19. But since she was wheezing, coughing and running a fever (all symptoms of Covid-19), Dabloo might also be infected, and he doesn't want to risk passing it on to his family.

Two hours later, when even though the sun has set its glow still illuminates the sky, Gudiya's parents, Bauji and his family, and Dabloo watch the fire engulf the little girl's body.

'Fire is the only element of nature that defies gravity, Dabloo. No matter how much you lower the burning log or candle, the flames will always rise towards the sky. So, no matter what pushes you down, rise up like a flame,' Bindu bhaiya had said to him once, in a moment of reflection while staring into a bonfire on a cold winter day near the field. No sooner had he said this than it had started to rain. They had run into the shed, and as they stood looking at the

logs of wood getting wet, bhaiya had said, 'And water, even when boiling hot, will always have the power to put out a fire. Keep your cool even in the most trying circumstances.'

As Dabloo stands here, participating in Gudiya's death—Gudiya, who was a stranger to him just a month ago—he wonders how many from her extended family would have wanted to see her one last time before they bid her farewell. It will hurt their hearts, as it hurts his to have missed Bindu bhaiya's cremation.

A cry rumbles from deep within his chest as he falls to his knees, touches his head to the ground and lets out a river of tears into the earth. Bhaiya's voice plays in his head, singing the refrain from the fisherman's song:

find me in those waters and all will be all right.

Take #20

A Resting Place

Mickey hadn't expected the flood of emotions he felt on seeing Sarita sing 'Megh Malhar'. *Sitara*,[39] as he'd called her when they were together many years ago, has become an overnight internet sensation. When he saw her video two days ago, it brought him to tears. It was as if her voice had breached the dam in his heart, reminding him of all their bittersweet exchanges.

The skies had opened up on cue, bringing the first downpour of the monsoon—like a force of nature. Each rumble of thunder took him further back in time:

'You've been reciting Ghalib's couplets to me all afternoon but when it comes to talking to Mai about our marriage, the cat gets your tongue,' Sarita had complained. She was resplendent in a rose-pink cotton

---

[39] Star.

sari as she sat on the floor of his friend's apartment, leaning against the sofa while he rested his head on her lap. His friend worked at an office in Nariman Point and often lent them his apartment on weekdays.

Mickey sat up suddenly, hands folded, and said, 'Sitara Devi ji, I have already told you that the day I sign my first film, I will enter your house with a baraat,[40] *no less. And if your mother or anyone else in your family offers any resistance, I'll make arrangements for us to elope.'*

'Be serious for once, Mickey. My family is looking for prospective grooms and I'm having a hard time staving off suitors. Some people in my family even think I'm a lesbian. It's only a matter of time before they plant that thought in everyone else's head and then I'll be forced to marry the next man wearing a suit and tie.'

Mickey chuckled. 'Who are these men your family is introducing to you, who wear a tie to a meeting for an arranged marriage? Are they visiting you during their office lunch hour?'

'You know how my family is. They are musicians, but they want me to marry someone with an administrative job. Just wear a suit, show up at my house and put your acting skills to use. We'll tell them the truth once we are married.'

Her tone was almost pleading. It wiped the playful smile off his face. No one was more precious to him than his Sitara and seeing her downcast made him

---

[40] Groom's procession.

promise that he would meet her mother as soon as he was back from his cousin's wedding in Delhi.

'I'll meet your Mai on one condition. You must sing to me every morning, afternoon, evening and night for the rest of our lives, and also any other time I demand it.' He played with the cascade of her hair that lightly brushed his face.

She bent forward to kiss him on the nose and said, 'You aren't my boss.'

'Not at all! In fact, quite the contrary. I'm the slave who's making his last wish with his head on the guillotine before he's executed. Isn't that the plight of men once they are married?' He winked.

Sarita slapped him playfully on the arm as he pulled her closer for a kiss. 'Let's practise starting now. How about you sing me something? After that, I promise to enthral you with more couplets.'

'That's a poor bargain but since that's the height of your talent, I agree to suffer it for the rest of my life.' She giggled and continued to sing.

Mickey closed his eyes to take in her honeyed voice, swaying his head and drumming his fingers on his chest. There was something about her voice that stoked the primal instinct in him. 'Let's elope right this minute!' he said when she finished.

Sarita's laugh was cut short when she realized that Mickey was serious this time. 'I have laughed off these suggestions earlier, Mickey, but our union is not just about you and me. It's about my family too. They are deeply rooted in tradition, and eloping would mean thumbing my nose at them. I don't want to bring them dishonour in any way. I'm fine with bending the rules, but not breaking them.'

What was to be two days in Delhi had extended to five. Mickey's uncle had had a heart attack the day after the wedding, and Mickey was kept busy with family responsibilities. So much had happened in less than a week; he knew he would talk Sarita's ears off by sharing all the details of his eventful trip with her. He called her as soon as he could but the moment he heard her voice on the phone, he knew something was wrong.

Sarita's news had rendered him speechless. She had been engaged to a man named Lokesh Mangeshkar. Her family had found out about their affair and all hell had broken loose. Mai had instructed the family to make arrangements for an engagement ceremony, and it had taken place three days later.

When Mickey got back to Bombay, Sarita met him at his friend's apartment. Pulling the scarf and sunglasses off her face, she ran into his arms with tears streaming down her face. 'The wedding is in ten days!' Mickey had always thought she would make a beautiful bride. But to imagine her as someone else's bride brought a lump to his throat. He hugged her, burying his nose in the nape of her neck; he wanted to hold on to her forever. He didn't let go until she pulled away, looking at him as if for the last time, before swiftly turning around to leave.

He prayed for a miracle. Each time the phone rang, he hoped it was his Sitara, telling him that the wedding *had been called off. The call he waited for never came but a common friend who attended the wedding told him she hadn't seen a sadder bride.*

The only way to prevent himself from going mad was to throw himself into work with a vengeance. If it took money (and a secure job) to make the world go round, he'd make sure the world of movies, at least, would orbit around him.

Sarita never contacted him after her marriage, and neither did he try to get in touch. And just like that, over three decades went by. As he watched the video of her singing the same raga a few days ago, he was transported back to that afternoon in 1995. His heart swelled with grief and a few hours later, he was clutching his chest.

The doctor at Lilavati Hospital said excessive smoking and chronic diabetes had blocked his arteries but Mickey knew better. It was seeing the bruises on Sarita's face. *Could her husband have hit her?* He wishes he could go to her but he's being given a drip.

There must be a reason he has survived the heart attack. Is life giving him another chance to meet and possibly reconnect with his Sitara? Mickey decides to reach out to her after he's discharged. He wonders if she knows about his heart attack.

* * *

In the wada below, the residents of Devri Chawl are still deciding which team should begin the first round of

Antakshiri,[41] before one of them erupts into a scratchy rendition of a Mohammad Rafi number. Meera steps into the toilet to hear Aditi more clearly over the noise.

'You already know how pitifully lonely Uncle has been after Aunty's death. We're all taking turns to spend as much time with him as possible,' Aditi says.

'Good on you for keeping him motivated.'

'I felt that pushing him to join hands with that local company that manufactures hand sanitizer would give him something to look forward to. You should have seen how relieved he looked when I offered to assist him with the distribution and marketing.'

'At least the work profile is up your alley, even if it's not the sector you want to be working in,' Meera says.

'I suppose it will keep me gainfully employed till I find a better fit. It'll also help me learn the ropes of running a business.'

'Will you be working out of Pune now?'

'Yes, though I will come to Mumbai to get my luggage.'

'I can't imagine living at our apartment by myself or with anyone else. I guess I'll move back to the women's hostel. The rent for the apartment is already coming out of my savings.'

'I almost forgot! Did you hear the news about Yashika Saini?' Aditi asks.

'Yes, I saw her post on Instagram announcing her pregnancy with her boyfriend. Congratulations have

---

[41] A singing game.

been pouring in on the *Bowled Over* WhatsApp group all morning.' Meera sighs, wondering what this means for the future of the film. While she's relieved that her role in the film is no longer in jeopardy, the trouble is, the film itself could be indefinitely delayed. With the pandemic and lockdown showing no signs of coming to an end, it doesn't seem like *Bowled Over* will cross the finish line any time soon. She must find herself a job before she runs out of savings.

'Your Patti sent me the recipe of her special rasam and asked me to make it for you. It's as if she's here without actually being here.' Manoj looks amused as she pours chai into two steel glasses.

As Meera walks towards the sofa, a sudden breeze sprays rain in her direction. 'You can shut the window if you like,' Manoj says, looking up from the besan pakoras she is frying.

'I'm quite all right with it actually. This reminds me of childhood monsoons in Chennai,' she says, sitting on a *mooda*[42] facing the courtyard. The torrential rain hasn't dampened the enthusiasm of the kids in the courtyard, who are dancing and jumping into puddles, even though the adults run for cover to the corridor. Watching the daily routine of the chawl's residents is an activity she has come to enjoy over the past four days. It's incredible how a change of place is beginning to ease her anxiety at having to heal alone during the

---

[42] A traditional low stool handmade in India from criss-crossed plant stalks and twisted rope.

lockdown. 'Patti would give me her special hot oil head massage, especially on weekends and rainy days, insisting it would prevent a cold. I hated it back then and tried to wriggle out of her grasp, so Patti offered to make rasam with hot papadam only on the condition that I sit still for half an hour. With time, I came to look forward to those weekend rituals. Isn't it interesting how we relate to people based on how pleasurable or painful our memory of them is?'

'That's true, dear. It seems that you have only pleasurable memories associated with your grandmother and she with you, given the way you both talk about each other.'

'That would be so. After all, we are each other's only family!' Meera bites her lip. Has she accidentally given Manoj an invitation to ask about her parents? To her relief, even if Manoj has realized her slip of the tongue, she does not show it.

'But does family mean only the people we are related to by blood? Isn't family the person or people we come to trust and commit our loyalty to despite the peaks and valleys of life? For some people, family may be those they will their property and assets to, even if they couldn't stand the sight of them when they were alive. But if you look at it, we humans are creatures of habit. And when people repeatedly reinforce their trust in each other through big and small acts, they can be called family, isn't it?' Manoj sips her chai slowly, savouring its flavour. 'My late husband and I never had children of our own. After his death, most neighbours here have become my people, and I've become theirs.

We aren't bound to each other but we have each other's back.'

Meera stands near the railing outside Manoj's tenement, overlooking the courtyard. Her memories of Amma and Appa have always been fraught with anger and sorrow. She's lived with these memories longer than she had lived with them. What if her parents were just a means for her to grow in the care of Patti, who has been both Amma and Appa to her? And then there are others who have come into her life for a reason or a season. Aditi, at first, just a flatmate, has become like family. Manoj has cared for her even though they were complete strangers. And Raghu, whose charming ways and possessive behaviour she'd mistaken for love. Yet, in this moment, it all seems to come together. Even though he's been her most challenging relationship, he has given her her biggest lesson in self-care.

Meera looks out into the courtyard, her face turned up to the pouring rain, and smiles.

* * *

Dabloo doesn't know how long he's been sitting by the side of the highway with his face buried in his hands. He hears the sound of tyres coming to a halt and looks up. The headlights of the van are blinding in the semi-darkness of dusk but he is so drained that even lifting his hand to shade his eyes is too much effort.

The driver and a passenger climb out, looking at the glowing embers of what was once a pyre, and then at the solemn faces around them. 'What happened?'

Tanju is leaning on Bauji's daughter-in-law's shoulder, her eyes half closed, lips moving inaudibly as if in prayer, while Dayaram is staring into space. None of them responds until Bauji, who gets up more to stretch his legs than to acknowledge the presence of the strangers, tells them about Gudiya.

One of the men pulls an ID card from his shirt pocket and says, 'I'm Prakash, a reporter with Samachar TV, and that is Kishor.' He points at the driver who is pulling the camera out of the van. 'We are on our way back to our Thane office and stopped on seeing you all. How long have you been on the road, and where were you headed when this incident happened?'

The reporters work their way through the 'migrants' (as Prakash mentions in a piece to the camera), before approaching Dabloo, who is sitting on the other side of the pyre.

'Are you also a construction worker?'

Dabloo shakes his head. 'I work as a food delivery boy.' He sighs, wanting them to leave, and does not make any reference to the film industry to avoid unnecessary questions. No sooner does the thought cross his mind than Kishor stops filming and whispers into Prakash's ears. They look at him, wide-eyed.

'Are you the actor Dabloo Yadav?'

How odd that a vernacular news channel crew would identify him, that too while reporting about daily wagers on a highway during the pandemic! Maybe they are referring to some popular theatre actor who happens to be his namesake because he's sure no mainstream actor has the same name. And if they've mistaken him for someone else, how short-staffed must news channels be to put their erstwhile arts and culture reporters on current affairs duty?

Dabloo nods half-heartedly, still confused.

'Sorry we didn't recognize you instantly, but what a brilliant performance you've given in *Ghummakad!* Hats off, sir!' They must have a keen eye to have recognized him despite his stubble and the dirt he's covered in, but how do they know about the film and where did they see it?

'Don't you know? Your movie was released on Amazon Prime almost three weeks ago, and it's been garnering praise and accolades ever since, especially your performance. In fact, our channel was trying to contact you but couldn't reach you. Now we know why.' Prakash nods at Kishor who positions the camera, possibly readying it to film their interaction.

'May I borrow your phone? I have an important call to make.'

Dabloo steps aside while the reporters speak to each other in low, excited voices. '*Pranam*,[43] Alka didi, my phone's battery died so I couldn't call you all these days. I started walking home; it was impossible even to stand on the platform. It's a long story, I'll tell you later. First tell me, how are Baba and Ma? And what about bhabhi and the kids? Please apologize to everyone for me; I cannot make it to the village just

---

[43] A form of respectful or reverential salutation before something or another person—usually one's elders.

yet. Covid is on the rise and I cannot put any of you at risk . . . Please don't cry, didi. I promise to visit as soon as the lockdown is over.' He looks at the reporters watching him and hesitates before saying, 'If there's an emergency, call me on this number.'

Although giving Prakash's number is an afterthought, Dabloo considers asking them for a ride back to Mumbai. They may refuse on account of the need for social distancing. But they also seem eager to interview him and might just agree to let him on board.

'I can ride on the cargo carrier.'

'It's an eighteen-hour drive to the studio and we'll stop only for toilet breaks. Can you handle it?' Kishor says.

Dabloo nods, hiding a smile. He has walked miles in the treacherous heat. Riding on the cargo carrier attached to the roof of their SUV will be a luxury!

'But before we head back, we'd like to ask you a few questions on camera.'

Gudiya's parents, Bauji and his family are gathering their belongings to leave. Dayaram is holding the tin box with Gudiya's remains. They exchange solemn namastes and Dabloo touches Bauji's feet. 'May you live long, son, and make a good name for yourself,' Bauji says in blessing.

Dabloo stands still, watching the group walk away, the distance between them growing. He would have waited till their silhouettes merged into the dark of the night, but he notices the red light of the camera blinking; he hadn't realized he was already being recorded. It's the first time the camera has made him self-conscious. He hears Prakash eloquently describe the plight of the migrants, which gives Dabloo a moment to steady himself. 'Even though life surprises us every once in a while, the pandemic has taken the phrase "truth is stranger than fiction" to a whole new level. Would you believe that in striving to bring you news and updates from the migrant exodus better than any other channel, we have chanced upon the star performer from the recently released film, *Ghummakad*?' The camera pans to Dabloo. 'Look at the turn of fate, Dabloo ji, you come into the limelight and are off-the-grid for the media and audience until we at Samachar TV find you walking back to your village in Bihar. What prompted you to make this decision in the middle of the lockdown?'

'My elder brother, Bindu bhaiya, passed away suddenly. I could not process the news when didi called me. In fact, I must have been in shock because I went to the Kurla train station despite knowing that the stations were chock-a-block. I was extremely close to bhaiya, so I was desperate to reach our village in time for his cremation. I tagged along with a set of workers and their families who were going to walk till they found a ride somewhere along the way. But that never happened, so I found myself walking all the way to Jhansi.'

'Our condolences. This must be an extremely distressing time for you and your family. Do they know you had set out for home on foot?'

'They were expecting me but I've decided to go back to Mumbai. Like I said, I had left in a daze but I'm concerned about my family's well-being now. Especially after some of the people I was with fell sick . . . and one of them—Gudiya—died. If I'm infected with the virus, I wouldn't want to put my family at risk too. We won't be able to handle another setback.'

'Dabloo ji, a little while ago when we were covering the last of Gudiya's cremation, and hadn't recognized you, you mentioned that you worked as a delivery man with an online food ordering app. What was that about?'

'That job was the only source of income I could find during the lockdown.'

'Did your family know about that?'

'No. Bindu bhaiya assumed that since the release of *Ghummakad* had been shelved a year before Covid happened, I would have exhausted my earnings from it. He insisted on transferring some money to my account initially, but I convinced him not to, because I didn't want to burden him with my expenses.'

'So how did you convince him that you could manage?'

'I told him that the production house I was working with was continuing to pay us during the lockdown.'

'Do you mean you were acting in a film?'

Dabloo shakes his head. 'I was working as a spot boy.'

This interview is like peeling an onion—the more the reporter asks him, the further back in time he goes until he's telling them about how Bindu bhaiya supported his decision to become an actor in the first place.

As the outside-broadcasting (OB) van speeds back towards Mumbai, Dabloo sees familiar landmarks flash past. He has walked this path before but he's not the same man any more.

Take #21

Take That!

Sarita turns up the volume on the electronic *tanpura*[44] to drown out the squall outside and closes her eyes to concentrate on her *alankars*[45] but she's not satisfied with her singing. Truth is, she hasn't been able to take her mind off the news she heard three days ago.

The phone rings, jarring against the notes of the tanpura. She opens her eyes. She usually remembers to put the phone on silent during her riyaaz but today she is as disorderly as the rain coming down from all directions.

It is an unknown number. 'Hello?'

'Sitara,' says a mellow masculine voice, then lets the silence linger between them.

---

[44] A long-necked, four-stringed instrument originating in the Indian subcontinent.

[45] A concept in Indian classical music wherein a vocalist creates any pattern of musical decoration within or across tones.

The wind is howling outside; it could well be the sound of her own anguish. She breathes deeply before saying, 'Mickey?'

'I got your number from Jayesh Bhayani. Is this a good time?'

'Good time?' she says and turns off the electronic tanpura. The way he's been on her mind for the past few days, it's as if she has manifested this call. 'How have you been? I saw the news about your heart attack but didn't know how to reach you.'

'I got discharged from hospital today. I was being driven home when I realized that the road past your house ends at my building. It's strange that our paths never crossed though we've been neighbours all this time. If only I had known!'

Sarita begins pacing the room when she hears this. How could he forget that, even when he *did* know about her engagement to Lokesh, when she had made a last-ditch attempt and begged him to talk to her family, he had done nothing? So what if they are neighbours? 'How does that matter, Mickey?'

'Of course, it matters! Do you want me to believe that the bruises I saw on your face in the video were from a fall you had? It's good Lokesh is already dead, else it would've been my hands around his neck.'

'How do you know all this?'

'Jayesh told me when I asked about you. I met him only recently and he didn't strike me as a connoisseur of classical music, so I did a double take when I saw your video on his TikTok account.'

Sarita wipes the fog off the windowpane. At some distance, from the swaying palm trees that line the periphery of her residential complex, she can see a fence of tall iron spikes, behind which lies Mickey's society. Through the rain, she can faintly see a part of one building. They must be a stone's throw from each other but their journeys have been so different. The man she knew about three decades ago had been painted as a bully by the media during the #MeToo allegation. Meanwhile, she'd suffered a bad marriage and sacrificed her peace of mind for the family's reputation.

'Sitara, that allegation is a storm in a teacup, but I don't blame you for believing the media. When you left to get married, I was shattered. I couldn't bring myself to truly love or open my heart to anyone.' Mickey pauses before speaking again, measuring his words. 'Life has been a continuous downward spiral as far as my relationships with women are concerned. I am ashamed to say it, but they became a means to an end for me. But I can't apologize for it in public; I'll have to just follow my lawyer's advice.'

It has stopped raining but the clouds still hover with the promise of more rain. Barring the slight strain in his voice, she hears the Mickey she used to know, who wouldn't sweep his flaws under the carpet. That Mickey always made sure to keep his communication honest, no matter how hot their debates got or how bad it made him look.

'Would you like to get on a video call?' he says suddenly.

She smooths down flyaway strands of hair before accepting his call. It's the first time in years she feels self-conscious about her appearance as she sees herself on the screen before he enters the frame.

His hair is like snow, not the salt-and-pepper look he had sported in photographs and interviews in pre-Covid times. He is pale—nothing like the distinguished, self-assured celebrity he's looked all these years. His shoulders hunch like he's carrying the weight of the world. The hooded eyes behind his spectacles seem to hold regret even as he smiles.

'Your voice still sounds as magical as it did. No wonder your video has gone viral. Looks like you've kept up with your riyaaz,' he says.

'Actually, I haven't, not as much as I would've liked to. I barely snatched the time when Lokesh went to work but that stopped during the lockdown. I'm creating a routine again now.'

She sees his mouth tighten. 'It's not my place, Sitara, but why didn't you leave him?'

'Sometimes there's a disconnect between what we want from life and what we resign ourselves to, Mickey. And I can object to some of your choices too,' she says, her annoyance reflected in her tone. 'I'm sorry, I didn't mean to judge.' *This isn't a time to grouse; his health is fragile.* 'I didn't mean to be harsh either. This past week has been rough.'

'I should've messaged first. I've been so overwhelmed since I saw your video that I called as soon as I got home. When can I call you next?'

His response puts her at ease. This is the Mickey she knew—attentive to her needs. They set up a time. The squall has passed and it's drizzling now. She opens the windows, lets in the breeze, and sits down to practise her alankars, which flow relatively better.

Mickey slides down in his bed. Is life giving him a second chance with his Sitara? She has good reasons for her reservations about him, especially after the beating his public image has taken. He can't undo the past but he is capable of course-correcting.

Sitara's presence is the only silver lining in his life, what with the stress of the #MeToo fiasco, the cancelled ASN contract and his heart attack. He must do whatever he can to make himself a better man for her sake. To do that, he'll need to give himself some downtime and take a step back from his duties as a casting director. In fact, the heart attack can be his reason for making a career shift.

Mickey strokes his beard, mulling over the options that will support his professional aspirations while still leaving enough time in his schedule for Sitara. Maybe producing films, or writing or sourcing stories? But maybe he's going too fast. He still doesn't know if she feels the same way about him, or if she would consider spending her tomorrows with him. His eyelids droop.

'You look fresh as a daisy,' he says, seeing Sarita in a floral yellow kaftan the next day.

She chuckles. 'I slept well last night and practised for almost three hours today. What you see is the look of satisfaction.'

'This reminds me of when we went to the audition of that play. Remember?'

'How can I forget? You duped me. I thought it was your audition, and they were being nice when they asked me to sing. It was only when they confirmed me as part of the cast that I realized what you'd done.'

'You refused.'

She sighs. 'You know Mai was dead against the daughters of the house joining the movies, and theatre is one step away from it. But now that I look back, maybe I should have taken the offer. At most, Mai would have reprimanded me or given me the silent treatment for a couple of weeks or forced me to quit, but I would have done what I wanted to.' Sarita's smile is thoughtful and melancholic.

'If you had the opportunity now, would you take it?' He waits for a response but is met with silence. 'I'll be frank because I don't know of any other way to be with you. I lost you once, and I don't want to lose you again. I want to have you in my life without making tongues wag. I know you've been through a lot and you aren't bound to say yes, but would you consider working on a project with me? It will give us a chance to get to know each other again.'

Sarita leans back in her chair. In the last few years, their relationship had begun to seem like a distant memory. *Within a year of her marriage to Lokesh, she was expecting their first child. The challenges of pregnancy took her mind away from the heartbreak she'd gone through with Mickey. All her waking hours were consumed in attending to her own needs and that of the life growing inside her. On days that were particularly stressful, she would sing to her baby to calm herself and walk around the house alternating between lullabies and classical ragas.*

But fate had other plans. She was at Mai's house when her water broke and she was rushed to the hospital. No sooner was Lokesh informed than he made a dash for the hospital. By the time he arrived, the doctors had declared their baby stillborn. She was spent, but Lokesh didn't even bother asking after her when he entered the room. After fleeting eye contact, he looked away and tailed the doctor out of the room, asking why they had lost the child.

In the weeks that followed, relatives from both sides called to express their condolences, some counselling them to go on holiday or on a meditation retreat, but Lokesh would have none of it. He seemed to have a bee in his bonnet about wanting to try again in a few months.

'But the doctors have warned of complications if we conceive before a year and a half from now!' she'd argued.

'Then we'll get a second opinion, and a third and a fourth, if needed.'

'That's not for you to decide, Lokesh.'

'I'm the father and I have as much right to decide as you do!' he said, his face looking like thunder. 'I heard rumours of your romance before we got married but your mother said they were false. But when you looked

so unhappy for a newly married woman, I knew you were still dwelling on the past. You should have sorted out your mess before agreeing to our marriage.'

'You know nothing about my life before our marriage so it's not for you to comment on. Besides, what has that got to do with losing the baby?'

'The doctor said that the mother's mental make-up during the pregnancy makes a lot of difference to the health of the baby. I bet that you let the disappointment of your failed romance come in the way of your prenatal care.'

'You're making too many assumptions! How can you accuse me of falling short in my maternal duties?'

'My parents want a grandchild, and they think I'm not doing enough to keep you happy. So, they're holding me responsible.'

'And so, you're dumping your annoyance at them on me.'

The constant bickering in the months that followed had led Sarita to believe that they were indeed in a loveless relationship. Bringing a child into this equation would only further complicate matters. At least without children, they could live under the same roof, presenting themselves as a couple during family functions, yet not be bound to each other by way of shared parenting duties.

As the years went by, Lokesh had become increasingly intolerant of her singing because it reminded him of the fruitless pregnancy. He didn't recover from that loss, eventually turning to alcohol.

It has stopped raining when Sarita decides to go back to her riyaaz. Everything looks clean and calm. The leaves are lush, sparkling with droplets of rain, as if they've been given a new lease of life. She feels enlivened after talking to Mickey. Is she ready to get to know him again? Is this life giving her a chance to make it work with him?

* * *

Thanks to Bidyut, Jayesh has been cast for the *Hy-Genie* hand sanitizer commercial. It pays to be friends with a casting director.

'Your upmarket house impressed them. I was lobbying for you to be the face of the brand,' Bidyut says, 'and when I mentioned your huge following on TikTok, they agreed immediately. Your contract now has a new clause that you need to post the video on your account to promote it.' *Bidyut knows how to be a good friend*. After the lockdown is over, Jayesh decides, he'll gift Bidyut a six-month membership at the gym.

He dabs concealer under his eyes as he gets ready for the shoot at home. Not only had Zainab helped him pick the right shade for his skin tone, but she'd also taught him how to apply it correctly. It's incredible how women can master something as complicated as make-up but draw a blank when it comes to men, who are so easy to understand. If only she could see how he felt about her! But he obviously hadn't made his feelings clear enough to get through to her stubborn head.

Jayesh's laptop is placed so the set designer can get a panoramic view of the room and give him instructions on adjusting the furniture and props for the camera. After some deliberation, she asks him to spread a bright-coloured sheet on the sofa. As he's lifting one side of the cushion to tuck the sheet in, he finds a Polaroid photo of a house party with fairy lights set against the wall. People's faces are blurred as if the picture had been taken in haste or on the move. The centre table is strewn with bottles of beer and glasses, and the ashtray is filled with stubs. He realizes that it's a photo of *his* house. The sofa and table are the ones he's dressing up right now for the shoot. The date is stamped at the bottom: 25 December 2019. He remembers travelling to Goa for a three-day shoot at the time. Zainab must have hosted the party in his absence but why hadn't she told him about it?

He sets the photo aside to finish tucking in the sheet when he feels something plasticky. He pulls out another Polaroid photo and as he sees it, his breath catches in his chest. It's the same date, and Zainab and Bidyut are locked in a passionate kiss. Bidyut has one arm around her waist and the other is cupping her breast. They look drunk and probably didn't realize someone had clicked them together. Somebody must have hidden the photo under the sofa and forgotten about it.

It's only when the designer calls out to him that he realizes he must have been glued to the spot for too long. Luckily, his back is towards the camera or the crew would have wondered why he looks like he's been hit by a ton of bricks. Jayesh slams the photos on the dining table off-camera, breathing heavily.

'Are you there?' the director asks.

Jayesh walks back into the frame, dabs on some powder, adjusts the cushions around himself and gives the team a thumbs up.

* * *

'The apartment has been shut for a while. It might be mildewed,' Meera says, strolling in the corridors of the chawl as she speaks to Aditi on the phone. 'I've decided to give it up; I won't be able to afford the rent for long. I've already spoken to the concerned person at the women's hostel and they'll have a room ready for me to move in next month. '

'Does Patti know?' Aditi asks.

'Eventually, she will. But I don't want to say anything to her at this point. She's already doing a lot for me, and I don't want her to dip into her budget for contingencies. If only I can get a job somewhere.'

'What kind of job?'

'I'll take anything I can find for the moment and keep auditioning on the side. Speaking of which, do you remember Lisa, the talent agent?'

'You mean "Fleece-ya", the talent agent? What about her?'

'She offered me an audition for a primary role in a digital soap opera, a twenty-episode series produced by Vishnu TeleFilms. They are a reputed banner, but the script is loaded with raunchy dialogue. Plus, the storyline is a rehash of other no-brainer shows.'

'If you make it to the final cast, don't expect me to watch the show! And what's with you attracting the sleaziest soap opera roles?' Aditi laughs as she asks the question.

'Beats me! I swore never to do a repeat of *Mera Parivar* but look at me now! My bank account is getting depleted and I'm desperate for a well-paying gig.'

* * *

Meera wonders how she'll audition at the chawl, given the perpetual noise. Shutting the door and window muffles the sounds but only a little. Manoj has been away all day attending to a client and will return late at night, so Meera isn't likely to be disturbed by any visitors.

Hair in an updo, she sits on the sofa, the only spot where her phone gets any signal. She crushes a pomegranate seed and rubs it on her lips and cheeks to give them a tinge of colour; the make-up essentials she'd ordered online haven't yet arrived because of the pandemic and she doesn't want to borrow from the ladies at the chawl because she has learned never to share make-up.

Meera knows the casting assistant Jiya from several TV commercials and cameo roles in web series, and wonders if she's working as an assistant during the pandemic out of compulsion or if this is how she's managed to bag so many acting roles.

Jiya says, 'My colleagues Aditya and Bala will be joining shortly to give you the cues for your dialogues. Any questions before we begin rolling?' She's busy filing paper, clearly not meaning what she's just said.

Meera decides to ask her a question anyway. 'Could you explain the context of this scene? I messaged Bala right after he shared the script but there was no response. The lines are vulgar; there must be a good reason my character is articulating that way.'

'Television writing is testimony to what's popular. This show will be a path-breaking one and is created by the makers of the long-running hit show, *Adhikar*. Have you watched it?' The icy undertones cut through Jiya's politeness.

Meera shakes her head. *I'd rather watch grass grow*, she thinks.

'The context here is how your character finds herself in a delicate situation when she's hit on by her husband's boss at a party. A massive business deal needs to come through, which could alter her husband's career graph. She's a trophy wife but bold and confident. She has to navigate this conversation carefully, telling the boss to stay in his lane. So, you see, there are many layers to her performance.'

How, in the name of women's empowerment, is Indian entertainment still passing off misogyny as 'path-breaking'? Meera decides to decline the project even if she's selected. But she'll go through with the audition, however perfunctorily. She's determined to infuse her character with as much dignity as she can muster. Something tells her that this project could very well go the *Mera Parivar* route.

'Varun has spent nights working on his skills. I'm sure he's better than anyone else . . . I'm happily married, Mr Rai. I'm not one for mixing my drinks—'

As she'd expected, Aditya and Bala break into chuckles in the very first take, distracting her and spoiling her expressions. They apologize but snigger like pre-pubescent boys in the second take as well, right in the middle of her dialogue.

'Stop it, you two,' Jiya says lazily. 'It's an inside joke, Meera. It's not you.'

Meera clenches her fist and inhales deeply. This is unprofessional behaviour at its worst. Maybe they've already shortlisted an actor for the part and this is just an obligatory audition. But even if it isn't, and they are yet to finalize her, it's possible that Vishnu TeleFilms will ask Lisa to intervene to make Meera lower her fee. In this case, Meera could earn more by working for a casting agency than being cast as an actor on this show or for any other breadcrumb roles. Even if it paid her a measly Rs 25,000 a month.

'You'll have to excuse me. I have a workshop to attend and I'm already late for it,' Meera says, logging off without waiting for a response. Even if she has just burnt her bridges with Vishnu TeleFilms casting, it feels like a weight has dropped from her shoulders.

'When you clear the clutter, you make room for new experiences, chellam. You did yourself a favour. I'm sure you'll get a great offer soon.'

'Actually, Patti, I've been toying with the idea of working with a casting agency. Mickey Taneja's studio has put out a hiring call for assistants for their upcoming project. I think working inside the system could teach me how to avoid the common pitfalls in an audition and help me get a role for myself. What do you say?'

'You know I can't give you even a paisa's worth of advice about your profession, but common sense tells me you might be on the right track. I can't tell you how many times I improved as a teacher by putting myself in the shoes of my students.' Patti smiles, revealing the small gap between her lower teeth, while her eyes look moist. This happens only when she experiences a bittersweet moment, usually something related to the distant past. 'I'm no mind reader, Patti, what do you want to say?'

'I am really happy you've found an alternative. I know it's unrelated but today, Shashi's servant came to help me clean the house, and when we pulled out the trunk from the loft, out came your favourite doll, the one you called Vasu for some reason. It was a gift from your Amma and Appa for your first birthday, and you treated her like a real person. Remember when her arm came off and you couldn't attach it back, so you stuffed a sock and asked me to sew it on her? I still don't know how you thought of that; you were only three years old. But that was a sign that you aren't one to give up on something or someone you love. I'm proud that you haven't given up on your dreams, chellam, and I pray to Lord Venkateswara that you never do.'

* * *

After the OB van turns in at the studio gate, everyone is made to undergo a Covid-19 test. Much to his relief, Dabloo tests negative along with the others, and the van is allowed to enter the compound. Once inside, reporter Prakash asks a peon to bring them tea and snacks, but Dabloo interrupts him. 'I'd like to wash up or take a bath, if possible.' He is taken to the green room and given a fresh set of clothes—a plain white shirt and navy blue pants—taken from the costume department.

He feels the warm water fall off his body, taking with it the grime and dirt of weeks and massaging his sore muscles. He is considering catching a few winks as he gets dressed when he hears a knock on the door. The peon walks in with a thali filled with dal, roti, mixed vegetables, rice, curd and salad. Dabloo is wolfing down his food while the monitor behind him plays his interview on repeat because of the buzz it has created since it aired the previous day.

'You've had an arduous journey thus far, Dabloo ji. What kept you going after the initial shock of your brother's death wore off?'

'At one point, all I was doing was walking, as if all this were happening to someone else, and I was just a spectator. I have felt hunger, fatigue and grief even *before the lockdown but nothing compares to this. It was Gudiya's death that pulled me out of my trance and I decided to return to Mumbai.'*

He is slurping up the last of the dal straight from the food tray when a man walks up to him and says, 'I'm Uttam, the editor-in-chief. Your interview has got very high viewership ratings. Can we do a sit-down interview and follow it up by documenting your return to your residence in Mumbai?'

Seeing Dabloo's eyes droop, Uttam says, 'I know you are tired but I promise, we'll wrap this up real quick.'

* * *

It's almost four hours later that the news van stops outside Dabloo's house, the camera already rolling. Though Prakash and the staff at the studio have been helpful and the editor-in-chief has prepared him for his homecoming being recorded, he feels as if he's shooting for a reality show about his own life.

Life is strange, he thinks. Fame has found him at a time when he's least expecting it; when he wishes to be left alone to make sense of all that has happened in the short span of a month. He climbs to the first floor, to the two-room-kitchen set he has been sharing with nine others. They and the landlord have been alerted about the news crew arriving to cover Dabloo's homecoming. His housemates greet him with broad smiles and claps. He almost doesn't recognize the landlord out of his usual T-shirt in a crisp shirt buttoned up to the collar.

'How does it feel to know that you've housed a celebrity for a tenant all this while?' Prakash asks the landlord who is only too eager to answer, surrounded by his wife, teenage son and neighbours, all peering into the camera.

Dabloo cuts through the crowd standing at the entrance to his house and goes to his room. He places his bag near the door, aware of the camera following him.

'Dabloo ji, you have gained a sudden and massive fan following since the release of *Ghummakad* and your interview with Samachar TV. Your admirers and fans now want to connect with you on social media. Any plans for joining a platform soon?'

'I haven't thought about it but maybe I'll start an Instagram account,' he blurts, more out of exhaustion and a desire to get done with the interview than from a considered position.

'One last question, what does your next career move look like? How do you see yourself taking your acting talent beyond the limitations of filming that the pandemic has imposed on the industry?'

Dabloo looks at his feet. They've carried him through some rugged terrain this past month—

'*Bhaiya, how long till we reach home?*' Gudiya *had asked, as she looked back at him from over her father's shoulder.*

'*Days, maybe weeks. Depends on how fast we can walk.*'

'*What if we ran? Would we reach in minutes?*' She *chewed at a fingernail, lost in a calculation of her own.*

He had laughed at her innocence at the time but now the memory of Gudiya sobers him. He may have brought her some cheer along the way, but she had taught him to look at life with a sense of wonder. And isn't that the greatest gift for an actor?

'Sir, I have spent eight years hustling for jobs in Mumbai and in just one month, I've gained recognition and appreciation from the public. I don't even know what tomorrow holds for me, but I definitely want to continue acting. For now, all I can say is that I'll put one foot in front of the other and go wherever life takes me.'

Take #22

No Character Is Entirely Fictional

It's one of those rare monsoon mornings in Mumbai when the sun has peeked from behind the clouds for just a minute. The light is perfect for making a selfie reel. Jayesh has just finished a most satisfactory workout and can't help but smile as the sweat shines on his shredded body. The endorphins are definitely helping him overcome the pain of the betrayal he felt on finding Zainab and Bidyut's photograph two weeks ago, on the day of the shoot.

Bidyut had called him days after the shoot and the first thing he had said was, 'The director was impressed with your home-video skills, but more importantly, with your professionalism. It's a huge compliment to you because he hasn't looked back since his independent film was selected for the Cannes Film

Festival. I told him, it's not for nothing that you're an influencer on TikTok and an artist in your own right.'

'Thanks for the recommendation.'

'Of course, bro! I believe the director is looking for a leading man for his upcoming feature. There's still time before the casting process begins but lobbying is a 24/7 job. Why do you think I cast you for this commercial? So that the director's team has some reference to context when I pitch you for the film.'

Jayesh gazed at the polaroid of them kissing as Bidyut continued to flatter him and promise him more work and so on. The photograph, held down by his sipper, had become soggy and wrinkled from being used as a coaster. He had been on the verge of tearing it into pieces a few times but would hold back at the last minute. On other days, he'd look down from his balcony and wonder what it would be like to jump off the building and put an end to his pain once and for all. The thought that held him back was the additional suffering he would go through if he survived the fall. There was also the added risk of being infected with the virus at the hospital. In fact, he was in such low spirits that he had even given his regular broadcasts on TikTok a miss.

Today, he's faring much better, which calls for a post!

But that's only if he's able to open TikTok—the app seems to have crashed. When closing the other tabs on his phone and even reinstalling the app and logging in doesn't work, he wonders if his account has been suspended. That's impossible! He's never violated their policies and had recently updated to its latest version which ensured bug fixes, and it was working fine. He restarts his phone but clicking on TikTok now shows the message 'network error' though he has full internet coverage.

Jayesh is still considering ways to revive his app when a friend shares a link on WhatsApp. It's a news article:

> TikTok among fifty-eight other Chinese apps banned in India over national security issues.

What? TikTok has too large a user base in India—it must be the other Chinese apps that have been banned. As he searches for the latest updates, he prays that this is fake news. But the results only confirm his fears. Jayesh sits still, unable to swallow another sip of his protein shake. Here he was, barely recovering from the blow of Zainab's infidelity, and life has dealt him another punch. What is he going to do? He was looking to capitalize on the number of TikTok fans he had. Even the *Hy-Genie* ad campaign was his because of Sarita's video going viral, boosting the impressions on his post. He had planned to approach her for another video collaboration and was waiting for the traditional mourning period to end but the Zainab–Bidyut revelation had thrown him. He wants to slam his fist into the wall. Instead, he directs his blows on to the cushion at the last moment.

* * *

It's only noon but the skies are dark. Mickey has been at his desk, struggling to put down a story outline for a feature film, but all he's done in the last three days is type words only to delete them later. As he stares at the skyscraper opposite his, the drizzle begins to look like the lines and specks in black-and-white movies, and the people in the building's window frames look grainy, as if they are actors being shot on a film reel in the 1950s instead of on a digital format. Maybe he should pick an old foreign film and remake it. Adding a plot twist to an existing storyline is better than building from the ground up. This way, he can delegate the work to his team, and only come in at crucial problem-solving and decision-making points. After all, if his plan is to transition from casting to producing and writing films, he might as well begin now. Besides, he has reached a position where he can allow himself time to attend to matters of the heart, both literally and figuratively. It's incredible how he's feeling a teenage excitement at the thought of rekindling his relationship with his Sitara. What's even more incredible is that she's just messaged asking how he's feeling. Talk about coincidences!

'Busy?'

'Just prepared my monsoon special, masala chai,' she says, sounding pleased. 'It's an instant pick-me-up!'

'Am I invited?'

Sarita pauses before saying, 'Aren't you supposed to be on bed rest?'

'I am, but I just wanted to hear your reaction.'

'Ha! The classic Mickey Taneja googly. Just like when you convinced me to sing at the audition you went for. I should have recognized that mock-serious tone. Some things just don't change.'

'Absolutely, just like you fall for it each time.'

'Jokes aside, you sound tired.'

'You know, Sitara, with the number of scripts and story pitches I've read and heard in my life, you'd think I'd be the last person to face a creative block. Yet, I feel like I'm pushing a rock up a hill in trying to come up with a story worthy of a feature film.'

'Maybe if you allow yourself time to rest and recover, you'll hit upon a good idea.'

'You're right, but I want to announce a new project soon to replace the #MeToo scandal in public memory. It was bad enough to lose the ASN contract. I don't want to lose projects at home as well.'

'That sounds far-fetched. I'm sure you've earned enough goodwill and support among people in the industry.'

'I heard from a close source that during the pre-production meeting of an upcoming film, the director dismissed my name when his team suggested it. Trust me, all goodwill comes to nought if the tide is against you.'

'What was the ASN project about?'

'ASN was going to do a show on struggling actors in Mumbai but Covid stalled the production. They saw a market in the sizeable number of aspirants who come to the city and those who nurture hopes for making the move but haven't taken the leap yet. I'd started to work on the show but then the #MeToo case made them back out.'

'Well then, maybe this is your chance to beat them to it.'

'What do you mean?'

'Remember what you said to me after we watched Dilip Gandhi's play which was adapted from a book? I think it was in the spring of 1994. You said, all original ideas are second-hand and it's only about how authentic you make them seem,' she says.

'But *B-Strugglers* is a reality series.'

'What's stopping you from fictionalizing it?'

Mickey sits up straight. *All original ideas are second-hand.* Sitara's right. He merely needs to reword the existing concept note of *B-Strugglers* to get started, and then pass it on to a team of writers to work on the nuts and bolts of the story. If all goes well, he could complete filming before ASN can even get the idea off the ground. Feeling energized, he opens his laptop, cracks his knuckles and begins typing—

Four struggling actors from different socio-economic backgrounds arrive in Mumbai and find that life in the film industry is beset with challenges. On one hand, a talented artist is struggling to make ends meet. On the other, a rich small-town person without talent will get what they want. Somebody else finds themselves being abused by someone in power, while yet another person is betrayed by their lover, jeopardizing their prospects of working in an A-list feature film and being abandoned despite being in precarious health.

Mickey looks at the cursor blinking on the screen, his enthusiasm dimmer now. The outline is missing the punch of a plot twist. What could it be?

* * *

In the two days since TikTok's ban, Jayesh has barely eaten, which has left him with no energy to exercise, breaking the daily workout streak he had maintained since the beginning of the lockdown. He tried reading a book but his eyes glazed over till the book fell from his hands. He then set out to sort his wardrobe by colour but halfway through, piled his clothes back as they were. He even tried posting a video on Instagram that he'd originally made for TikTok, but it wasn't the same thrill—the likes came in trickles and there wasn't a single comment until an hour later. Just when his TikTok following had begun to grow in spades, fate had dealt him a cruel hand. Those numbers were his currency for gaining roles in films and TV commercials.

Meera's call interrupts his thoughts. She must be calling to request a rent cut again, which he is in no mood to entertain. No sooner does the ring stop than she texts him, giving him the mandatory months' notice before vacating the apartment. Great! Even the rental income he's making from the apartment is going to stop. Aditi's notice period is almost over; she's just waiting for the lockdown to end so she can collect her luggage. And now this.

Pappa was right: 'One needs money to make more money.' But there's no way he's going to join the family business full-time. Somehow, he'll just have to make things work for himself in the movies.

He is lying on his sofa staring at the ceiling fan when he gets the reminder for this evening's masterclass. He had enrolled for Mickey Taneja's acting workshop, hoping that it would put him on the latter's radar and bring him meaty acting opportunities. Mickey had been conducting the sessions himself during the lockdown but since his heart attack, the classes are being offered by other stalwarts and upcoming professionals.

Logging into the virtual class, he sees thumbnail images of the participants and is surprised to see Meera as the moderator. What a jump—working for an NGO to taking an acting masterclass! Was she one of those actors or agents who give false profiles so they can be eligible tenants? He wonders if her call a few months ago was to cast him for a project instead of a request that he reduce the rent as he'd assumed. But she would have texted him if that were the case and she hadn't.

Meera says, 'It gives me great pleasure to introduce Dabloo Yadav as your acting coach for our three-day workshop, "No Character Is Entirely Fictional". We've seen him in *Ghummakad* and have been inspired by his effortless portrayal of Murtaza. But did he model his character on a real person? What are the techniques to make a character believable? We'll dive right in and let Mr Dabloo take us through the steps of creating relatable and compelling characters.'

Jayesh hasn't watched *Ghummakad* but looking at Dabloo, he wonders if he'll have to start paying more attention to his building's watchman. Who knows who could turn out to be walking red carpets and doling out acting advice to him in the near future? How were such plain-looking actors getting primary roles?

'There's not much difference between what's real and what feels real. In fact, there is no difference. Both are tricks of the mind,' Dabloo says. 'Let me give you an example. Imagine you have to pass a sleeping lion and the slightest movement you make will wake it up, and it will devour you when it wakes up. What are you going to do? You'll walk on tiptoe, clear objects from a path carefully, use sign language or whisper to anyone around, and even hold your breath when you see the slightest movement or hear the least sound from the sleeping animal. Every action will be pronounced. The actor's task is to keep his attention on what he is doing and make the imaginary object or experience as real as possible. To do that, one must train one's five senses because all human responses come from sensory experience. In all of this, if the lion wakes up, you'll either freeze or run for your life. Now imagine you have a gun or tranquilizer to protect yourself. Would that make you less afraid? Would that change your behaviour or body language as you pass the sleeping lion? So, you see, acting, just like life, is the see-saw between what is and what can be, between what's real and what's imaginary.'

* * *

Mickey has just finished speaking with Atul Kapoor, the producer of *Bowled Over*.

'The market is down, and investors are wary of putting their money on high-risk undertakings like movies. They won't agree to their investments being blocked indefinitely. Cinema halls are closed, and it's not like people are going to flock to the theatres as they did in pre-Covid times even if they reopen. I don't want to discourage you, Mickey, but hold off turning producer till the situation stabilizes,' Atul said.

'Goddamn this virus,' Mickey mutters as the Covid-19 death count flashes on the news ticker tape. While one channel reports that the virus has originated from the wet markets of China, another pins the outbreak on a lab leak intending to unleash bio-warfare on the world. Bio-warfare or not, it's ridiculous that the domino effect of Covid-19 that originated in Wuhan can affect the laws of the land in other countries—to the extent that even a Bollywood film producer is talking like a gloom-ridden market analyst from a business news channel.

But people won't stop making or investing in films for good. He strokes his beard, mentally sifting through his connections in the industry. He knows enough producers and financiers, but something tells him that he needs to look for a novice with deep pockets—someone who's eager to get a foot in the door. The trouble is, most of the novices he knows are actors, who are not exactly made of money. *Unless.* He turns off the television. He knows exactly whom to call.

* * *

'Good evening, Mickey sir.' Jayesh answers the phone on the first ring.

'Are you busy?'

'Not at all! I just logged off from the acting workshop with Dabloo Yadav. Today was the third and final day, and also the best! The part where he asked us to correlate our individual journeys in the lockdown to our emotional memory as actors was incredible.'

Mickey makes a note of 'actors in the lockdown' on his laptop and says, 'We've signed Dabloo for some advanced level workshops also in the coming months. There are limited seats so make sure you register well in advance. But I'm calling you for something else. I'm producing a feature film and it's not just any feature film—it's a meta-film. A genre I will be among the first to explore in India. I'm in talks with an OTT giant who's excited to begin work. They are insisting we cast A-listers for the main parts, but I disagree.' Mickey pauses, trying to heighten the suspense. 'I'm looking for a fresh face since this is a story about aspiring actors. There are many to choose from, but I want someone willing to put skin in the game. Would you be willing to finance your first break in the movies, Jayesh?'

Mickey is smiling when he disconnects. He might just have given the term 'casting coup' a whole new meaning. The actor on his first film as producer will also be its financier. And that's not all. It feels like he has hit the jackpot by finding a supreme twist to the tale of *B-Strugglers*. Like his good friend Jerry from ASN had once said to him, 'One can never tell when people's realities become more interesting than fiction.' Mickey pulls a cigarette from the drawer. *There's nothing more satisfying than beating someone at their own game.* He types:

Four struggling actors from different socio-economic backgrounds arrive in Mumbai, but the pandemic dictates a change of plans . . .

Mickey reads and re-reads the finished document, his eyes sparkling at the thought of going on floors with his most ambitious film, *Take No. 2020.*

III

Cut!

Epilogue

2022—A Double Take

The waiter brings the ice bucket holding the champagne towards the table on a trolley. Glancing at the actor who essays the role of Dabloo for permission, he pops the bottle open. As Dabloo begins to speak, all eyes turn to him. 'Each time I'm in Venice, I make a stop at the *Ristorante Antiche* where the Dom 2006, Maison Ruinart is arguably the best champagne I've had. When I made the reservation, I told the maître d'hôtel that we would be celebrating our film *Take No. 2020*'s premiere. And especially after the reception we got yesterday at the Venice Film Festival, we must raise a toast. Who'd like to go first?'

'After the screening,' says Mickey, 'everyone was calling us by our characters' names. That, in my opinion, is a testament to the impact the story and our performances have had on them. Here's hoping our characters always outlive us as actors.'

The others cheer loudly. 'Hear, hear.'

Atul adds, 'Even at the press interviews, all I heard was compliments about the film's production values. But the best part was when a lady couldn't stop gushing at my acting prowess. She kept saying what a multifaceted person I am.'

'You're a star, Atul uncle!' Meera is vivacious. 'I've grown up hearing dad tell me how, even as a producer, you gave him more acting suggestions for his scenes than his directors did. It's surreal that I'm the one acting in a film with you, not dad.'

Atul runs a finger through his slicked-back hair, looking pleased. 'You should have seen that lady fawning over me after I told her I had written some crucial points into the script. Like the part where I send Meera's character in a vanity van instead of a cab.'

Sarita blows a ring of smoke in the air. 'Being a producer in real life as well, it must have been easy to get into the mindset of the character.'

Atul says, 'When one has worked in the film industry as long as I have, each talent naturally starts flowing into the other.'

Meera leans in. 'The only similarity between my character and me is that her motivation to be an actor came from home—growing up with Patti who is so keen to explore her creative side, and also from reading her Amma's stories which fuel her imagination.'

Jayesh leans close to Meera, whispering, 'You have your dad's acting talent, by the way. Who would believe this is your debut film? Let's hope we are paired together soon. Our chemistry will set the box office on fire.'

Meera makes eyes at him as she clinks her glass to his. 'Cheers to that!'

An Italian woman approaches Dabloo gingerly. '*Mi scusi*,[46] I don't mean to intrude but I'm a huge fan. Can I get a picture with you, please? I just cannot get over how beautifully you expressed the anguish of Dabloo, especially when you're being interviewed by the reporter while sitting on top of the OB van. Even though you maintained your composure outwardly, there was such a restlessness in your eyes. So many actors develop tropes with time but even your superstar status has not jaded your performance.'

Dabloo smiles. '*Grazie*!'[47]

She shifts her gaze to the others. 'Are we going to see a sequel?'

'We can drink to that!' Mickey replies, raising his glass.

The woman leaves after a few selfies with them.

Jayesh asks Dabloo, 'I must ask how you prepared for the scene on the OB van.'

'I have specific playlists for each mood and for that scene, I plugged in the melancholic one, which got me in the groove.'

---

[46] Excuse me.

[47] Thank you.

Meera joins in. 'It worked. I had goosebumps. Actually, just thinking about it makes me tear up now.' She dabs the corner of her eye. 'After watching the rushes at the studio, Dad was busy heaping praise on your performance till I asked him, 'What about me, Daddy?'

When the laughter dies down, Sarita taps the ash off her cigarette and says, 'I have to agree with your dad on that. But also Gudiya—her performance was a show-stealer. If only she were here too!'

Jayesh nods. 'Her parents did not want her to travel long distances, especially after the news that children are more vulnerable to the new variant of Covid-19. I shot for a commercial with her three years ago, so I've been in touch with her parents since.'

Atul reads aloud from his phone: 'Patti regrets having to miss today's dinner. She is slightly unwell and is resting in her hotel room.'

Meera says with a hint of a smile, 'Oh! I forgot to tell you all. Even Manoj isn't coming. She went dancing at an after-after-party last night and I believe she's still hungover.'

Sarita quips, 'She and Lokesh should have been paired together for this movie!' before bursting into peals of laughter.

Atul says, 'Now, *that* would have been a casting coup, given they dated each other a long time ago.'

Sarita says, 'But casting, in general, is an amusing process. Just the other day, I received an audition call to play Akshay Kumar's mother even though I'm younger than him by over a decade!'

'Did you take it?' Atul asks.

'I said what Dabloo says in the movie: I'll take whatever comes my way.' She winks at him. 'Nonetheless, it was fun ribbing the assistant. He told me it was for a period film, so I asked if it was a sequel to Akshay Kumar's film, *Pad Man*. The guy didn't get the pun. He explained that period means a story based on a historical event.' She spills some wine on herself while laughing.

Mickey doesn't join her. 'That poor assistant would've quit if he had to endure even half of what I've gone through with you pulling pranks on me during the shoot.'

Sarita says, 'My character was in such a dark place. I had to use humour to stop myself from going insane. And then there were strict Covid-19 protocols we had to follow too.'

'Same, aunty.' Meera's voice has lost some of its excitement. 'Especially in the later scenes I had with Raghu. I even had to take a few therapy sessions after the shooting was complete to get them out of my head. By the way, where is he?'

Raghu and Aditi bustle in. Jayesh waves at them. 'There you are! We were just talking about you. I thought you were going to give this dinner a miss.'

Raghu apologizes for being late. 'Thank you for holding our seats. We caught two more screenings today—one French and the other Polish. Then we couldn't find a cab for twenty minutes because it's so busy during the festival.'

Aditi says, 'A young film-maker offered me a role in his indie feature film saying that my artistic services will be paid for by the exposure I'll get. Can you believe it? It's 2022 for crying out loud! I excused myself, saying I had a press interview to give for my film's premiere here. You should have seen his jaw drop.'

Jayesh shakes his head. 'You would think the pandemic would have awakened people's conscience but what do you know? 2022 is nothing but 2020 too!'

'I thought the standing ovation we received would have made the news already,' Atul says.

'They clap for anything at these festivals—'

Raghu bites his lip as the table goes quiet for a few seconds, before he continues carefully, 'I mean, the real test always comes from a ticketed audience, doesn't it?'

Everyone looks at their plates.

Mickey says, 'Pass me some of the tagliatelle.'

'Tah-lya-tell-eh,' Dabloo corrects him. 'I learnt it at a pasta-making workshop during an earlier visit. My instructor began the workshop with an interesting remark. He said, 'Cooking is an adventure where you, the hero, must overcome unexpected obstacles to reach your goal, the perfect dish. And when you can't make a good enough dish, make a good enough story to go with it. Because at the end of it, we're all just gluttons for tales.'

* * *

Acknowledgements

The day I finished writing my book, I forgot how to write altogether. Thereafter, even so much as framing a creative sentence would sometimes feel as painful as pulling teeth. It made me realize that had it not been for the people who helped me while I put enough sentences together for it to eventually be called a novel, I would never have gotten to the point of penning my gratitude here.

It started with my mother, Cheena, calling me from a literature festival (in the year 2018 or 2019) and spelling out her wish to see me author a book someday. Even though I've been a writer for most of my professional life, I never thought writing a book was up my alley. And so, while I politely noted her comment, I brushed it off in my mind as an exercise for the second half of my life perhaps. I'm quite certain that it's her prayers that sowed the seed for this reality.

In 2020, at the cusp of the lockdown, I came to Delhi from Mumbai, thinking it to be a matter of days before I returned to the grind (like many others). Days became weeks, weeks became months, and while working on a project, I found myself dreaming up a storyline completely unrelated to the one I was crafting. Before I knew it, there were post-it notes all over my room—I was collecting the bones of a story and little by little, filling it with its flesh, fire and lifeblood. I knew I was doomed once I started journaling from the perspective of my imaginary characters.

My father, Harinder Sikka, has been and continues to be a source of massive support to me in all aspects, but he especially helped on the days I needed to vent about hitting a wall with writing. *It takes one to know one sometimes.* But on other days, if by the end I looked like I'd been hit by a bus, he would nonchalantly ask, 'How many words did you manage today?' and that would honestly make me want to bury myself underground. It was too hard to quantify each day's work. With time, I've come to appreciate how different we both are in our approach to the same task, and yet have a similar and natural affinity for the self-flagellation that writing a book entails.

My brother, Samar Sikka, strolled into my room once, casually inquiring about my progress. In our regular conversation, he mentioned a common practice in the film industry that sparked an idea, giving the story its compelling end. For this, I'm forever grateful. On days when our conversation has had an agenda, he has been an ally—sharing inputs and ideas on marketing the book or putting his weight behind the project to ensure its success.

If someone can look at a *subpar* first draft and still not judge you or your calibre, they must be deemed a friend for life. Raul Chandra was a sounding board for many creative outbursts on my part. He even proofread the first draft of my book for spelling, punctuation and grammar, for I had naively assumed that if I had gotten to the end of the book, it must be good enough to be submitted to whoever was looking for manuscripts.

It was Vinita Zutshi who gleaned the potential of the story from the hot mess of a first draft I had presented to her. An author, editor and friend for many years, she mentored me chapter by excruciating chapter, patiently teaching me the skill of *show, don't tell* in storytelling among other gems, and brainstorming with me when setting up the tent-poles of the story and everything in between. Engaging with her was like participating in a workshop on fiction writing. It helped me understand how I needed to remove myself from the story—much like in life, where we must get out of our way to get somewhere.

Vallery Puri, the artist who painted what has become the cover design of the book, was a benevolent stranger whom I had cold-called one afternoon in 2021. Based on the synopsis that I'd shared with her, Vallery got to work over the months, sending me sketches and updates as she added paint, patterns and textures, and her signature magic to the canvas. In all of this,

I've come to understand that as beautiful as her art is, it is also a reflection of her spunk and spontaneity as a person.

I must thank Kasturi Kanthan (KK to me and her countless students at Lady Shri Ram College), who so generously lent me her surname, Kanthan, for Meera and shared her insights into Tamil culture. She and Vinita Bhatnagar were my Sunday reading companions during the lockdown and the first few people who lent me an ear and words of encouragement as I narrated the story one Sunday (despite the fact that it was gobbling up Vinita's sacred siesta time).

I'm grateful to:

Rahul Nanda, Rakita Nanda, Girijesh Goud (the golden man in the book), Dr Savita Sekhri, Dr Dimpy Gombar Amit Palit, Kanishka Gupta (my agent, Writer's Side), Ipsa (the editor I worked with from Writer's Side), Vaishali Mathur (my editor, for accepting my manuscript and giving it an audience), Aparna Abhijit (the copy-editor, for helping bring more nuance to the storytelling), Shadab Khan (the designer, for good-naturedly going back and forth with me on the title fonts and colours) and many others who've given tangible shape and form to the book at Penguin Random House India.

I'm so thankful for the support of my family (including extended family) and friends who've offered me unwavering support and positivity, and held space for me on occasions when I thought I'd lost the plot (in life, not just in the book). Not to forget my German Shephard companion, Simba, who has been my source of joy and the object of my affection all through, and especially during the lockdown. He can't read or offer counsel, but he can understand better than any human that a calming presence alone can untangle so many knots—I cannot begin to describe the peace he brings in the storm. He's so precious.

They say, 'The price of anything is the amount of life we exchange for it.' In that regard, *Take No. 2020* is my most special, creative baby. Enough said. Now on to learning to write again!

Scan QR code to access the
Penguin Random House India website